– Liverpool –
MMXXIV

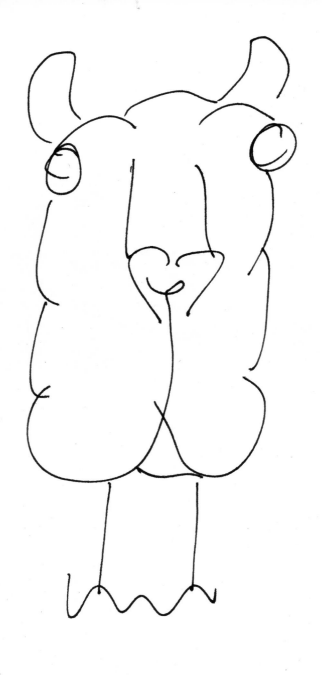

THE MUSLIM COWBOY

Drew,

yalla / yeehaw!

[signature]

dead ink

First published in Great Britain in 2024 by Dead Ink,
an imprint of Cinder House Publishing Limited.

Print ISBN 9781915368386
eBook ISBN 9781915368393

Cover design by Emma Ewbank / emmaewbank.com
Typeset by Laura Jones-Rivera / lauraflojo.com
Editing by Gary Budden

Printed and bound in Great Britain by
Bell and Bain Ltd, Glasgow

www.deadinkbooks.com

Supported using public funding by
**ARTS COUNCIL
ENGLAND**

Funded by
UK Government

MIX
Paper | Supporting
responsible forestry
FSC® C007785

THE MUSLIM COWBOY

BRUCE OMAR YATES

dead ink

To Charles

I

SHANE

Somewhere in the desert of Iraq a man with light brown skin sits up from a thin mattress in the dark of a concrete room and speaks English, and he says, 'Oh boy...' The mattress is patterned, though the colours are faded, and a dirty white pillow lies hollow at its head. The man sits bare chested in silence and a white sheet hangs down from his lap. Outside, the land is level and hard and old and dark, and it too sits in silence though of a different kind, it having given birth to the first of most things and the man to no such firsts.

After a while the man stands wearing only a pair of loose white boxer shorts. He is not yet of middle age but he is already a man, though he is without a moustache or beard. His eyebrows are joined in the middle and his shoulders are evenly set, and his stomach is flat and his legs are long. The room is cold and the man walks to its centre and crouches. He clatters a small pot over a movable gas stove, steadies himself, and sets water from one of two plastic bladders to boil, then he returns to his mattress and collects the white sheet. He wraps it over his shoulders and head and moves across the room like a wraith. He takes water from the pot and runs it over his head and his arms and his feet, then he rolls out a mat and he prays in dips and bends.

Afterwards the man lounges with the sheet on a concrete bench above his bed. He is now dressed along with his boxer shorts in a light blue denim jacket unbuttoned to show his hairless chest, and a tin cup of hot coffee sits next to him and steams on the bench. In one of his hands is a Koran from which he reads in silence, and in the other is a thick vape pen which he sucks at in long tokes. He billows thick streams of vapour from his mouth and nose which hang above him in clouds and wisps, and the rising sun begins to cast a pale yellow glow on the room through an open window. Soon the man collects his belongings and loads them into a large rucksack of black nylon and rolls up his prayer mat and fastens it to the top, and then he looks this way and that.

Eventually the man steps out from the small concrete shelter as a silhouette against the impossible orange grey dawn sky. If he were visible beyond the flatness of that dark shape it would be noticed that he is now dressed in trousers of the same light blue denim that makes his jacket, and that under his jacket is a white shirt with a collar and the buttons undone at the neck. In one hand and over the shoulder hangs his nylon rucksack and in the other he lifts a heavy wooden piece with four legs tied to it with string and a large cushion. In dark and battered army boots the man pads over the dust towards the dark outline of a prone camel. When he arrives the camel yawns and nods its dangled head as if in greeting.

The man bends down and fastens the wooden piece in place as a saddle on the camel, and to that he fastens his luggage. The camel huffs and then sits patiently of fat and fur with its long legs folded as if in incubation beneath it, and soon a pair of leather straps sit snug under its throat and its tail. The sun makes long shadows of the stick of the man and the blocks of the camel and the building which stretch and move quietly together across the flat land wide and in flickers. The man returns to the room and then steps out again, this time with the patterned mattress rolled like his prayer mat and his two plastic water bladders slung over his shoulder, and these too he fastens to the saddle.

When the man is ready he lifts his leg up and comes to sit down on the back of the camel who for its own part makes a great heave forward and then back and then raises itself and its heavy load and totters until it stands level. Now balanced on top, the man half turns at his waist and reaches a hand behind to where a dusty black media player set in a speaker of a prior generation is fixed to the back of his saddle. He presses the wheel of the player and the song 'I Never Cared for You' by the singer Willie Nelson begins to play in stanzas and strums. The man lifts a dirty beige felt and wide brimmed cowboy hat and fits it on the top of his head. Then, because the man knows the morning is cool and the day ahead will be hot, he speaks an instruction in English without delay to his camel, whose name is Hosti, and he says, 'Giddy up, Hosti.' When the man speaks in English his words come out strained in an accent locked between the Arabian stop and the American drawl, and when he kicks his heel to the belly of his beast it moans and it walks.

The man and his camel ramble then slowly through an unparticular portion of the naked desert which is pathless and brown and of gravel and dust. As the sun rises to its full intensity the man sees his shadow stretched out and warped before him with its hat and its collar and its camel, and throughout that morning and afternoon he indulges in its outline as its owner. They trudge baked beneath the hot sun until at some point from under the brim of his hat the man squints and sees hovering blobs of darkness that emerge from the dirt and then begin steadily to grow and wobble on the horizon. After a further stretch on the same path the man and his camel make their arrival at that horizon manifest, and it becomes clear that the objects of their approach are neither blobs nor hovering but large structures of metal. Another stretch and the pair reach the structures and then start to pass them, and while the camel slogs forward and pays no concern to the spread that surrounds them, the man, swallowing the greater depth of his acknowledgement, notes that these are the abandoned tanks of an army.

The tanks sit heavy and large in long rows that stretch out to the distance on either side. They are uniform and each made up of a flat metal head resting low on a chunky metal duck breast which in turn carries fat grinding wheels that are wrapped in thick caterpillar treads. From the head of each machine protrude various complications but most evidently the long snout of a cannon, and written on the side of each piece are stencilled letters that spell 'US Army' and lines of serial coding.

The man looks down the row of dilapidated tanks as if into a pair of parallel mirrors and watches the metal duck breasts and snouts recur infinitely off into the desert. Their colour is light brown in camouflage for the landscape, but many of the tanks in their abandonment have become appended with various shapes and scribbles of graffiti which say words like 'Wisdom' or 'I Heart U' in English, and 'God Protect Us' or 'Glory Be To God' in Arabic. The ground around is littered with metal and plastic and is a deeper shade of brown having been dug and upturned when the vehicles were arranged there some time prior.

Beyond the belt of rotting tanks are the limits of a grey compound flat and wide. The man and his camel ride on to it and come face to face with a row of thick concrete blast walls packed side by side in a long line and which stand twenty feet tall. The man looks up at the wall and then left and right and sees it stretch off and around on both sides as if surrounding the compound. He pulls his camel sideways to tread the perimeter and after some time on a ride there they come to a great entrance.

They stop for a look before the man encourages his camel to ride through and then to trace the inside of the wall. They go dwarfed by the wall to their left and now giant rusted silos on their right before they meet a path that turns inwards and follow it deeper into the enclosure.

Inside is a borough of metal and concrete barracks which have been left and now bake under the hot sun. The man and his camel ride along roads of dirt which twist and turn to define neighbourhoods of maybe a thousand buildings with walls and roofs of thin metal lined with the same concrete slabs that make the perimeter, but smaller. The man brings his camel to cover the extent of the abandoned camp until they know it's entirely empty, and when they reach again the great opening of their arrival the camel is made to go prone in the shade, and finally the man climbs down.

The man lifts his hat to wipe sweat from his forehead and brings his vape pen from his jacket pocket and tokes. He holds and then blows a thick cloud of vapour and then replaces his hat and walks to examine a row of the barracks. Gaps in the blast walls have been left to expose grated stairways that lead to thin metal doors, and each lever on each door is marked with an old red tag which is sun bleached and printed with the word 'Vacant'. The man sees a metal bar on the floor nearby and puts his pen away. He begins to whistle a cordial tune and moves to pick the bar up, then he climbs the nearest stairway to the nearest door and swings the bar at its lever in clangs which resonate against the concrete blast walls until the lever is hacked off, then the man opens the door and steps inside.

Inside it is cool and the man allows his eyes to adjust. The light from the sun shines through the dusty windows and illuminates the faded room. Several metal bunk frames lie stripped and naked behind old metal footlockers. The man whistles his tune and wanders up to the closest footlocker and reaches as if with performed insouciance at its lid with his bar to lift it. It is empty and he lets it fall shut again. He looks up and sees a row of empty metal shelving units, then he readjusts his grip on the metal bar and returns outside.

Throughout the rest of the day the man moves from door to door and barracks to barracks whistling and scavenging by this example. By the evening he has turned out a box of golden tipped lithium batteries which he takes and a crate of bottled Coca Cola for which he praises God, and he spends the last of his energy to haul the crate back to his camel. The sun has begun to set in the distance beyond the concrete walls of the forgotten camp and it paints the vast sky a gradient of purple shades and brings sharp angled shadows to the streets of the old barracks, and the flat land that spreads unlimited beyond the great walls lies still and happy as it cools.

Hosti the camel teeters now and moans, and the man apologises and lowers from its back the heavy pack and saddle. Then he removes a bottle of coke from the crate and lifts its lid with the edge of his pen from his pocket and drinks. The coke is warm and sweet and the soda tickles his dry mouth and bubbles in his stomach when he swallows. He holds the bottle up close to his nose to study it and again praises God, then he tips it up to show the label and drinks as if to down it but the gas stirs him up and he has to stop and hang his head for the hiss. He cries tears and waits for the air to come back through his throat until Hosti moans again and the man still bent lifts the bottle up and behind him to the camel who takes it in its mouth and tilts its own head back in turn and empties it.

That night the man sits cross legged against the wall on his thin patterned mattress which he has laid over a bunk in the corner of the barracks. His denim lies slung over his saddle at the foot of the bunk and he wears only his white shirt which he has tucked into his boxer shorts. The man swigs dreamily from another coke bottle with his face illuminated in blue by the screen of a portable disc player which sits on his lap and hums black and unbranded and ugly and foldable and beaten from travel. The film on the player is *Once Upon a Time in the West*, an old film starring Charles Bronson and Henry Fonda which was directed by Sergio Leone and released many years ago. The film has two storylines that take place around a town in the old American West, the first a battle for land to do with the construction of a new railroad and the second an old crusade of vengeance against a cold blooded killer.

The man had for a long time argued with himself about which was the greatest film of the American West since he first happened upon a locker of discarded titles in an unparticular town in a time before, and as he had been left with little in the world to take his attention since the war, he had submitted himself through days and nights to their stories as he only knew how until over time there had grown in him an unquestioning possession. He had gone on to ride spur and rein with John Ford and John Wayne through films like *Stagecoach* and *The Searchers*, with Clint Eastwood through *A Fistful of Dollars* and *High Plains Drifter*, and with those and many others through films like *Red River* and *Rio Bravo*, and *The Magnificent Seven* and *Man of the West*, and so on. And so the man went and so had he gone, and trampled had become whatever doubts recent history might have impressed on him until whether the man liked it or not he had fascinated for himself a second faith.

And in those films the man hadn't only seen the distinct templates for good men and bad men and for a life of questing and justice where actions could lead to clear consequences in contrast to the many ambiguities that had been imposed on him and his country of late, but he had also seen the template for the life of a survivalist, and though his favourite characters were maybe of ignorance and self-indulgence they were also of fairness and honour. And it was those characters who had seemed good men for him to learn from and those films that had become practically applicable to living in a land that had long been operating on the raw logic of survival.

And the man sits and watches *Once Upon a Time in the West* as he has before but newly this time with the joy of warm cola, and caffeinated to fullness there he thinks that the slow pace of the film with its sparse dialogue and brief bursts of sudden violence is a truer representation of real life than that shown in other films he has seen, and he thinks that the filmmaker must have been far more interested in that which surrounds the bursts of violence than in the violence itself, and then in a scene that leads to the film's climax Henry Fonda's character Frank and Charles Bronson's character the harmonica man talk over the building of the railroad and their voices are tinny in the disc player as they speak, and they say how they're from an ancient and emotional race of men unlike the railway tycoon Morton who is from the new breed of businessmen with all his pragmatism and detachment, and how the new breed will displace their old ways of principle and imperfection so that nothing will matter anymore, not land and not money. The man watching thinks how the harmonica man is perhaps the character in the canon of his collection with whom he most identifies, and how there's something of melancholic nobility in the transcendence of the moment he's just watched, when suddenly he is jarred by a noise from outside.

He pauses the film and looks beyond the screen to abstraction until he hears far away rains of rifle fire and the deep pop of a distant explosion, then he rises and sets the player aside. He reaches his arms through the sleeves of his jacket and steps out into the night where he dips his bare feet into his boots, then he moves down the stairs and onto the dust where Hosti the camel is stood spooked and moaning. The man looks up and sees the crescent moon which hangs in a dome of unnumbered stars. He studies their clusters and patterns for a moment but he isn't an astrologer so he sees no more meaning there than anyone else might.

The pale light has delivered the whole camp as if into a pool of luminous blue. The man approaches his moaning camel and looks at its flat head and sulky pout and into its large dark eyes. He offers it comfort in touches and whispers and the camel settles and spits. There are further rattles of rifle fire and resonant pops of distant bombs. The man stands at the limits of the camp and looks out beyond the great blast walls across the vast dark desert. The source of the noise is a red glow that flickers on the horizon. The man looks at the glow and strokes the cheek of his camel, and thinks that he would rather be back inside with the resumption of his film. He is too far away for the glow to light up his face in red or to reflect in his eyes, so he just stands there and watches in the pale blue darkness.

The next day the man and the camel ride early ahead of the heat, and they pack their belongings and pass through the great opening in the camp barbican long before dawn. Good ground has been made by the time the sun begins to rise, and when the man looks back like the wife of Lot he sees that the walls of the city and its belt of abandoned tanks have already been sucked into the horizon and are long gone.

When the sun rises to fullness it brings its heat unsheathed like a sword, and then the two begin to sweat and the man lifts a pair of sport sunglasses scavenged at a time before to the bridge of his nose. Soon the two discern a road which emerges from the gravel beneath them as if to break the surface of the dirt like a whale having come up from the ocean to lift and carry them along on its back. After having travelled along the road for a while they pass a sign on a metal pole which is a red bordered triangle with the silhouette of a camel on it. By then the sun has more or less reached its zenith so the man says, 'High noon,' and they stop and sit together under the shade of the sign and share a bottle of coke between them in sips.

They sit and they doze and Hosti spits and the man tokes from his vape pen a strawberry flavour which fills his head with a haze of pink sweetness which is cool and thick, but soon the man thinks that there will be no ground made if they aren't the ones to make it so he climbs back on the camel and is lifted and they wander on. Once again they steam and sear over the road which has for them cut a path through the vast desert plains of Iraq, and after a while the man begins to notice a litter of empty cans for energy drinks on the ground. Soon after that there are thick dark track marks all around them, and the man thinks it looks like the dirt has been disturbed by a number of fast and heavy vehicles, and he thinks too that the desert with its wind and its sand hasn't yet had time to cover up and reclaim the tracks for itself, and that means they're recent.

As they proceed along the road the tracks multiply until the man and his camel are travelling small and slow on the road as if surrounded by the ghost of an army. A wind picks up and brings with it some cloudiness which turns the sky white, and the man removes his sunglasses and with a chill he thinks of the fiery glow on the horizon the previous night.

Eventually the man and the camel reach a small town which sits half trampled and burnt and left smouldering under the white sky. It looks as if the tracks have run straight through and all the way over it rather than around it. The ground is peppered in plastics and rubble and broken glass and energy drink cans, and the buildings made of sandstone or brick are there quiet and pale beneath patches of dark soot. In one tower taller than the rest a fire still burns and the windows have popped, and thick black smoke billows up from it into the sky.

The man and the camel ride deeper into the ruined town and pass a single charred tree that stands naked amid the rubble. The man sees various graffiti still visible under the soot on many of the walls which are thick scrawls in Arabic of black and blue and a wall of green stencil, along with a large damaged black and white poster which depicts a pair of white-bearded men in black turbans, one who looks sidelong and the other who peers ahead with solemn intensity, and the man recognises these bearded men as the former and current Ayatollahs who are leaders for Shia Muslims.

The man then notices a crumpled black banner on the ground ahead. He rides to it and encourages Hosti the camel to go prone, then he climbs down and examines the banner which has green text written in Arabic on it. He half turns to his camel and speaks English in his difficult American Arabian drawl, and he says, 'This is a Shia town, Hosti.' The camel looks away and moans and the man pulls his vape pen from his jacket pocket and adds, 'At least it was.'

The man raises the pen and clicks the button on its side to activate its vapour when a loud crack rings out and startles him and forces his free hand to his hat. He looks around the street to find the source of the noise when another crack rings out. The camel moans and rises to its feet and staggers and stumbles to the side of the road. The man notices movement then in a small cloud of dust on a street corner some feet in front of him and cries out and runs to see what it is.

He turns the corner and sees a red metal door on a house there slam quickly shut to send another small cloud of dust into the street. The man stands and looks at the door and then takes caution and steadies himself. He looks the building up and down and sees that it is a concrete house of two storeys, then there's another great crack and this time a flash of light at the man's feet. He jumps and flings his vape pen into the air with a yelp and loses his hat, then he stands unstirring for a moment with his eyes closed expecting the worst. Nothing else happens and when he opens his eyes dust is coming to settle around his boots.

He looks around again as he bends down and picks up his hat. He beats the dirt from it and places it back on his head, and there on the ground beside where it was he finds a triangular pocket of thick brown paper about half the size of his palm burst and blackened around the edges with burn. He lifts it and brings it close to his nose and smells charcoal and sulphur. He turns it over and diagnoses it as a firecracker, the kind for a child to light and run from or to slip under the chair of an adult while they sleep. The man thinks that things like firecrackers were more fun in the old Iraq than in the new where loud pops might imply far more than fun and laughter, and then he drops the burst firecracker on the floor.

Still kneeling the man looks up at the house and as if in performance at the opportunity of an encounter he puts a hand in his hip pocket and pulls out a square of red fabric. He ties it around his face like a veil leaving only his eyes exposed, then he looks to the side where his vape pen has landed and puts a hand on it and struggles to his feet. He turns the pen over and holds it up in both hands like a drawn revolver with its snout to the sky at the side of his head, then he brings it down and aims it gravely at the house, and with one hand he tilts the brim of his hat and walks slowly over to the red door. He stops and brings his ear to it and the metal is cool on the side of his face. He strains to listen but hears nothing, then careful and sweating he reaches for its handle and finds the door unlocked and opens it to be ajar. He readjusts his grip on the vape pen and steadies himself and takes a breath through his veil, and then with a rush he kicks the door and it swings fully open.

THE MUSLIM COWBOY

* * *

The man stands and looks into the dark house as the door bounces away off the inside wall with a clang and returns slowly with a creak. He holds his vape pen up to the side of his head and with a surge of spirit steps over the threshold, pointing the pen like a revolver in front of him into the darkness. He blinks hard until his eyes adjust to the gloom, and once recovered of sight he scans it in earnest.

Several thin patterned mattresses are spread along the dirty white walls over a concrete floor, the rest of which is covered by a rug of deep red. There's an electric heater in one corner and a potted kentia palm in another. Near the far wall is an opening into a hallway, and beside that is a low table with cups for tea and a pot and a strainer. Against the adjacent wall is a glass cabinet of books and magazines along with a framed photograph of a family. Depicted is a thin older man in a shirt and waistcoat, a pretty woman with light eyes wrapped in dark sheets, two boys in tracksuits branded with pictures of Mickey Mouse, and a baby which is presumably a girl since she is dressed in a soft pink cotton babygrow. The baby girl is the only subject looking away from the camera, and instead she looks at the elder of the two boys.

The man looks at the photograph and thinks for a moment about the cartoons of Mickey Mouse when there's a noise and from the corner of his eye he sees a small shadow scuttle through the hallway past the opening in the far wall. He quickly turns and points his vape pen at the opening, but all is still. The man edges towards the opening and when he reaches it he sees a stairway that leads up into darkness.

The man looks behind him where the hallway seems to lead to a kitchen, and then he turns and ventures carefully up the stairs.

When he reaches the top he spins quickly around the corner and points his vape pen out into a thin corridor. The walls are dirty white like the room downstairs and there's some light from a window at the corridor's end. The man sees that the coast for the moment is clear so he pulls his vape pen up and drags and blows from under his red veil before pointing it back out in front of him. When the vapour fades he sees two doors on the right of the hall and that the window at the end looks out onto the adjacent house. He inches his way to the first door which is ajar and kicks it lightly with a booted toe. It swings softly open and the man puts his back up against the door frame and then pokes his head into the room.

The curtain has been pulled to the side which allows light in. The room is stark and contains four uniform beds with thin mattresses a few inches thick on thin wooden frames. Two of the beds are side by side so they look like one double and the remaining two are positioned irregularly as if they otherwise wouldn't have fit. One of the remaining beds beside the window is unmade and underneath it is a cardboard box of red and other colours with the words 'Happy Boom' written in English and then some safety information written in Arabic. On the box is a picture of Jerry the mouse from the Tom and Jerry cartoons, and the man thinks again about American cartoons and of mice. The box is full of small triangular firecrackers like the one the man found exploded outside.

THE MUSLIM COWBOY

The man pulls his head back around the door and with his back to the wall looks down the corridor to the next door which is closed. He creeps silently towards it and puts his ear to it and listens but hears nothing. He readjusts his fingers around the vape pen to ensure his grip on it is solid, then he takes a deep breath and at once curling his lips and tensing his stomach he swings open the door and flies into the room with his pen pointed out into the dark.

He spins around searching wildly for an enemy but there's nothing in the room besides an empty plastic clothes horse so he relaxes and exhales and lets his vape pen drop with his arms to the side, but his next intake of breath brings a thick smell beneath his veil and through his nose and mouth which fills the whole of his head, and it is rank and tyrannical and deep and sickening. The man inundated with it stifles a cry and then gags and retches and falls to his knees.

In front of him is a bed and on top of it lies something human shaped and wrapped in white sheets. The man looks on and winces at blowflies that tick and crawl across the sheets and jump and land and disappear into the folds. The smell is constant and biting, and hot and rotten and as cloying as cheap perfume.

The foulness of it brings the man in reflex to cup his veil to his mouth and nose with one of his hands, but still the smell gets through. Then he remembers his vape pen and fumbles it in a panic to his face. He hurries the snout beneath his veil to his mouth and tightens his lips around it and inhales deeply. He billows thick vapour out through his nose and then brings more to his mouth from the pen without delay. The cavern of his head fills with the sweetness which disguises the smell in the room, and so using the pen as a purifier he goes on.

The man slowly approaches the bed leaving a dreamy trail of vapour in his wake and studies its length. He walks its extent from the tail to its top. The human shape is lightly wrapped in its sheets and the man pauses beside what should be its head and looks at it. Vapour trickles up and away from his nostrils as he removes his hat with his free hand and presses it to his chest in respect.

A corner of the sheet is loose next to what should be the head and a blowfly crawls underneath. Although the liquid that fills his pen is without nicotine or any other tonic and serves more as a lightweight and carriageable hookah, the man feels a light fuzz in his brain from the lack of oxygen and the walls of his vision start to bend. As he stands there and sways he puts his hat back on and then swaps his pen to his left hand to keep it propped in his mouth. He snores another cloud out through his nose which floats down and disperses then he looks down through watery eyes and slowly reaches out to the corner of the sheet with his free hand.

As he takes hold of the sheet the door behind him shuts with an almighty slam. The man jumps nearly out of his skin and fumbles his vape pen. He chokes on the vapour and coughs and flaps and falls backwards to the floor with his legs in the air, and then from the floor and through his whoops and splutters he hears a lock turn in the door and a pair of light footsteps scatter down the stairs.

* * *

THE MUSLIM COWBOY

The man rolls around and finds his hat and puts it back on his head, then he pulls himself to his feet and pockets his vape pen. He considers the locked door and the footsteps and then once more he tastes the room and his eyes close and he winces, but he shakes the flavour from his head and readies himself with a step back and then he charges at the door. The door gives way with more ease than he had expected so he floats through and with surprise and some panic on his face he slams into the wall in the corridor beyond. He peels himself back and races along the corridor holding his hat to his head until he reaches the top of the stairs and then below he sees the back of a young girl make a flash for the landing. At that moment a noise begins to rumble from somewhere in the near distance.

The man turns and makes for the first bedroom where he swings the door open and puts a knee on the bed at the window, then he holds the curtain to one side and looks through into the road. He sees nothing but can still hear a hum, so he presses his cheek against the glass and looks sideways in the direction from which he had himself approached the town earlier.

Back beyond the buildings with their graffiti and the rubble and the single blackened tree the man sees a black humvee truck roll into view. A great cloud of dust rises up from behind it and men in black overalls with automatic rifles stand tall in its bed next to a large fixed weapon. One of the men tilts his gun up and sends a loud round of ammunition into the ashen sky, and a heap in orange who must be their prisoner shivers and shakes at his feet in the bed of the truck. Just then, the red metal front door slams downstairs, and the man at the window lets the curtain fall and leaves.

When he comes outside the man sees the young girl running from the house as fast as she can and follows her to the corner of the street that turns into the main road where he knows the humvee will make its approach. He thinks that it might now be four hundred metres or so from the girl, and he runs faster so he can stop her from meeting it. He catches her up and sweeps her into his arms and lifts her back around the corner to the house, and he hopes that the men dressed in black won't have seen them because he knows what those men do and he knows it is bad.

The girl struggles in his grip but even a skinny man is too strong for a young girl and he carries her tightly as the hum of the truck grows closer and louder. He reaches the red door and drags the girl inside and throws her down, and with a hand on her arm he pulls the door to but leaves it ajar so he can look through the gap. The humvee reaches the junction at the corner and stops. Its brutal frame shudders and its motor growls and putters, and then with a great rattle it goes silent and the man's heart reaches his mouth and he brings the door shut.

Inside from the end of the man's arm the girl calls out in a small voice and he pulls her close in a hug and cups his free hand over her mouth. She is light brown like him with dark hair to her shoulders and of eleven or twelve years old, but clearly still a girl, and not yet a woman and not yet between girl and woman. Her legs kick and twist in dirty blue jeans with bare feet, and she pulls at his grip with thin arms in the dirty sleeves of a white cotton blouse. Finally she calms and the man takes the chance to listen for sound outside in the road like a footstep in the dirt or the open or close of a door, and the girl is silent and still as if she too listens with him, but they hear nothing. Then the man hears a small noise like a soft lapping and wrinkles his eyebrows to focus. He quickly realises that it's not from outside and falls away grossed and gurning from the girl who with her tongue has licked the inside of his hand wet, and he hangs his mouth open in disgust.

The girl takes her chance to run for the hallway, but the man falls forward and reaches for her ankle and takes it and brings her back to the ground. He jumps on top of her and puts his knee on her chest, and pushes her into the rug and cups his hand to her mouth again. He hushes with his free forefinger to his veil and pleads silence with his eyes, but the girl wriggles and squirms as before, and through his hand she bluntly moans, and then they hear the door of the humvee slam shut outside.

The man and the girl freeze together and both give an abstract look up and behind them as if through the wall and into the road. They lock eyes and the man glares at the girl who has stopped squirming. He slowly removes his hand from her mouth and she stares back at him cautiously and remains silent. With another face of disgust the man wipes his wet hand on the jeans of the girl, then he looks up at the door and then at the window. He gestures for silence once more and then crawls across the room on his elbows and knees to the window. He touches the windowsill with his hands and slowly raises his head until he can see into the street. The small girl on the floor hesitates and watches the man in his hat and red veil, then she too crawls to the window and does the same.

They can see the humvee stationed in the middle of the road at the junction. Stood next to it having climbed down from the passenger side is a sturdy and strong man with light skin dressed in a long black cotton robe with buttons at the neck. Trousers from a black pyjama meet his black boots underneath, and a bullet-proof vest hangs open over his shoulders. His face is chiselled and nestled in a light brown beard at the chin, and there's the suggestion of a moustache on his upper lip and rimless glasses on his nose. His hair is short and a black glock handgun hangs in his hand by his side. He stands and his chest pulls his robe taut and makes spread the vest across his shoulders. He looks around at the rubble with eyes vacant and glazed.

As this strong man seems to contemplate the area two others in black overalls jump down from the back of the truck. One wears a round cap and the other a moustache and a thin black bond on the top of his head, and both have light brown skin and are bearded at the chin, with dark rings around their eyes and automatic rifles that hang from straps on their shoulders. Their detainee who's tied by his hands and feet wears full orange and has a brown bag over his head, and he sits on his knees in the bed of the truck and makes a great shudder at the sound of their boots hitting the dirt in scrapes, before settling into a shivering anxiety as the men pad away from the humvee and into the road.

From the window the man and the girl watch as the men in black overalls wander back past the trampled banner on the ground and approach the graffiti walls and the damaged poster portraits of the bearded Ayatollahs. The strong man in his black robe watches them go and then turns slowly to regard the trampled banner. The man with the cap begins to scrawl red script over the ruined posters and the other with the bond watches, and the strong man moves to the banner with his handgun still at his side. At that moment in the empty stretch of road between the back turned strong man and the bag headed detainee in the back of the truck Hosti the camel trots silently with dangling head in hops and bobs from one side of the road to the other. The man at the window cringes and nearly cries out but the camel turns around a corner and disappears without having been seen. The man puts his forehead on the windowsill and softly exhales.

The strong man stands over the banner and observes its script for a moment. Then as if boiled to sickness he spits on it and exclaims a single word in Arabic, and he says, 'Rejectors,' which is a word that when said in Iraq and in Arabic has grown in stature to mean a great deal more than simply to say those who reject. As the strong man looks away he sees the recent footprints of the man and his camel in the dirt.

The strong man crouches down and touches one of the boot prints with the barrel of his handgun and then looks up. His gaze follows the prints to where they disappear around the corner of the street. With eyes honed he rubs the dust from his handgun on his robe which leaves a light mark on his hip. He looks up and behind at the men in black overalls and then back to the corner of the street as he rises to stand, then he puts his tongue to his teeth and issues a sharp whistle.

The man in the cap stops painting and he and the man in the bond both turn to attention. They take up their rifles and approach the strong man who follows the boot prints to the corner of the street. The prints come past the window through which the man and girl inside are watching and the two dip down below the frame to avoid being noticed. The pair lay there silently as the strong man passes on the other side of the wall.

The man inside gazes from their position under the window along the wall and across the dark corner of the room to the red metal door at the front of the house, then he looks at the girl and points with a finger to nowhere in particular but with allusion to the road outside and in English he quickly speaks, and he says, 'Bad men are in the road.' The girl looks at him with scrunched eyebrows and her eyes move from his face to his finger and back again. Her eyes are glassy and green and he senses that she doesn't understand his words. He pulls his veil from his mouth and lets it hang around his neck and he speaks them again, and he says, 'There are bad men in the road.' The girl looks at the man's face and then at the window and again scrunches her eyebrows, and then the black overalled men in the cap and the bond walk past the window and the man and girl both see them and recoil. The man hurries to his feet and takes the girl by the arm, and they run into the hallway and up the stairs.

They enter the first room with the thin framed beds. The man leaves the girl who stands at the door and goes to sit sideways on a bed beneath the window. He eases the curtain aside and looks down onto the main road. He can see the parked humvee at the junction and the orange man knelt in the back next to the large fixed weapon. He can see the strong man who stands now at the corner of the house to study the boot prints that run around the corner to the red metal door and he can see the men in black overalls, and again he says, 'Bad men.'

He beckons the girl over to the bed and she sits on it. He points down at the soldiers and then looks at the girl and draws his thumb across his neck as if to slice it and then closes his eyes and sticks out his tongue. The girl looks at him and holds out an open hand palm up to gesture out the window and raises her eyebrows with the kind of condescension only a young girl can show and she engages him twice verbally with downward inflection, and she says, 'Ali Babas.' And he looks back and says, 'Ali Babas?' And she says, 'Ali Babas.' And he says, 'Ali Babas!'

The man stands up from the bed and sinks into the room in thought. The girl watches him and he scratches his head under his hat and wipes his face and looks this way and that until his eyes fall on the box of firecrackers by her feet and his eyes widen and he throws a finger to the ceiling. The girl brings her feet up onto the bed and the man falls to pick up the box and then stops. He looks out the window and thinks, then he puts the box on the bed and looks at the girl. He gestures with his hands and speaks English again, and he says, 'Stay here.'

The girl raises an eyebrow and the man glides out the bedroom and back down the stairs and over to the potted kentia palm in the corner of the front room. He reaches into the pot and pulls out a handful of large pebbles. He looks briefly at the red metal door and then pockets the pebbles and sprints back up the stairs and back into the bedroom where the girl is still sat on the bed. He looks out the window. The strong man has now vanished around the corner to the front door and the men in black overalls are headed the same way. Meanwhile yet another man in black overalls and a long beard and sunglasses has opened the humvee on the driver's side and hoisted himself up to attention, and this sunglasses man watches the others over the roof of the vehicle.

The man at the window looks at the girl and points at the box of firecrackers, and in his Arabian American drawl he says, 'You got a light?' The girl looks at the man puzzled and then losing patience with him speaks Arabic, and she says, 'I don't understand you!' The man looks at her and winces and then hurriedly picks one of the triangular firecrackers from the box and holds it in front of her face, then he points at the thread wick and makes a sizzling noise with his tongue. The girl slaps her forehead in understanding and points at the ceiling, and the man looks up.

The girl leads the man out of the room and towards the window at the end of the corridor. The box of firecrackers is under his arm. The man waits while the girl reaches up to undo the window's latch. When the girl presses her palms against the bottom pane to lift it up there are three loud knocks on the red metal door downstairs and the pair freeze.

The man and the girl look back down the corridor and then at each other, then the man drops the box on the floor and they break into action to work the window open. The man looks behind again, and when he looks back to the window he sees the dirty soles of the girl's bare feet rise up and disappear beyond the top of the window. He pokes his head out and looks up, and he sees the girl on a set of steel bars fixed to the wall of the house as a ladder leading to the roof.

The man brings his head back inside and crouches over the box on the floor. He takes a handful of firecrackers and stuffs them in the pockets of his jeans. He reaches down for more when he hears the great clang of a boot against the metal door ring out from downstairs, and then he is outside on the wall and the window is kicked half shut and he is on his way rung by rung to the roof of the house.

He reaches the top and pulls himself up, and then falls over the berm there and rolls onto the flat surface of the roof. The girl kneels at the opposite ledge looking down. The man wriggles furiously across on his stomach until he is beside her and then brings his head over the threshold and looks down.

Below them is the red metal door. They see the strong man take a few steps back from it and stand in the road between the two men in black overalls. He looks at the door and then he draws a circle in the air with his finger and tells his comrades in Arabic to scan the perimeter of the concrete house, and the two men start to walk in opposite directions around it, the cap one back around the main road and the bond one through an alley at its side.

The man looks at the girl and she turns to her left and points to a rug at the edge of the roof adjacent to them. Laid on the rug is a pair of chunky galilean binocular glasses on a neck cord next to a big box of safety matches. The two of them keep low and move across the roof to the rug where the man kneels and empties his pockets of firecrackers and pebbles. He looks over the ledge onto the main road and sees the humvee in the middle of the junction with the sunglasses driver and the orange man, and below them sidling along the wall he sees the cap man. Then from the roof he looks across the road at the opposite houses and those too are concrete with flat tops and in various states of charring or disrepair.

The man ducks back from the ledge and pulls his veil back up over his face. He picks up the box of matches with a picture of two rearing horses and their riders holding cutlasses and pulls out and strikes a match and brings it to the wick of a triangular firecracker.

The girl is back at the ladder looking down. Below the metal rungs and the window is the alley, and she sees the man with the bond come around the left corner to investigate. He scans the walls and sees the window half open and spots the rungs that lead up to the roof, and the girl ducks back so as not to be seen. The man in the cap comes around the opposite corner with his rifle in his arms and the man in the bond silently beckons him over. When they're together the bond one whispers something in the ear of the cap one and points up to the window, but as the man in the cap looks up a great crack sounds out and startles them both, and they run to the corner of the alley to look out into the main road.

At the junction something pings noisily off the chassis of the humvee. The driver in sunglasses jumps down and dips back inside the car, and the orange man starts and moans through the bag over his head. At the front of the house the strong man steps away from the door and penetrates the humvee with a look of perturbation, and at the back of the house the men in black overalls duck into the alley and hold their backs against the wall. The man on the roof takes another match from the box and strikes it and touches the flame to the fuse of another firecracker.

It sparks and he throws it and it sails silently over the road and onto the roof of a burnt out house opposite. He picks up a pebble from beside him and waits again until the firecracker bursts with another loud crack, then he quickly stands and flings the pebble at the humvee. It connects and another great ping rings out, and the man looks on from the roof as the driver with sunglasses wobbles in the front seat and reaches over to the door on the passenger side. He frenetically pops the latch on the window and pulls it down and shouts words in Arabic, and he says, 'Watch your heads, there's a marksman on the roof!' And he makes a gesture to indicate the rooftops on the opposite side of the road while the poor prisoner exposed in the back of the truck moans and squirms to make himself as small as he can.

In the alley next to the house, the girl sees the two men in black overalls press their backs tighter into their position against the wall and ready their rifles. The one with the cap in front searches the rooftops on the other side of the road when another great crack rings out and another ping comes off the chassis of the humvee, and then the man in the bond shouts out in Arabic, 'It's an ambush!'

Startled by the noise and the uproar, Hosti then runs moaning from an opposite alley, and unthinkingly the men in black overalls react to send short bursts of rifle fire to rain in the camel's direction. Their rounds miss the camel whose neck and head hang lolling and nodding at the top of its lumbering trot and hit the ruined walls behind it to send chips of stone flicking and flying into the air. The camel huffs and lopes through the cloud of dust and then turns at the next corner and prances away down the next alley.

The strong man sees all this from around his corner at the junction and presses the bridge of his nose between the thumb and forefinger of his gunless hand, and he cringes and boils and then shouts and speaks Arabic, and he says, 'You idiots, what are you waiting for? Start the motor!'

The driver wearing sunglasses hurriedly pulls the window up and bolts the latch and sits in the driving seat and ignites the machine and the entire thing bangs and roars and shakes into life.

The girl watches as the men in overalls leave the wall at their corner and turn back down the alley with their heads down, and from the roof she follows them around to the other side of the house where the strong man is. The humvee rumbles and churns and thunders and the orange man falls like a sack to his side. The truck stirs the dirt beneath it as it turns and comes rocking to a stop at the house in front of the strong man who pulls open the door and jumps into the passenger seat.

Then there's another crack and a greater ping than ever before from off the top of the humvee, and the men in black overalls flinch and then launch themselves into the bed of the truck next to the orange man. They keep low and there's a shout, and the motor bangs and the brutal thing sends dust into the air and rounds the junction at the edge of frenzy and at last departs and hums into the distance.

The man and the girl on the roof look at each other. The man pulls his veil down and smiles weakly as if to draw a line under the episode, and then he turns and walks to the ladder and leaves the roof. The girl looks after him and then stands and follows, and she goes with him through the house and down the stairs and out through the red metal door. As the man emerges he takes off his hat to pat it for dust with two heavy strokes and then he puts it back on his head. Then he walks the rest of the way to the junction as if in parade with his fingers in his pockets and his thumbs at his belt. The girl watches and follows. The man stands in the middle of the junction and looks in the direction the humvee has gone. He spits but it isn't thick and it doesn't go far, and he frowns at himself and then casts a glance back at the girl.

He brings his thumb and forefinger to his lips and whistles with upward swing, and Hosti trots out from an alley between two decrepit concrete walls and skips loosely over in a romp. The man receives the beast with a few clicks of his tongue and strokes its neck, and then dives into one of the smaller pockets on his black nylon rucksack and brings out a handful of small plastic vials which are liquid refills for his vape pen. He chooses a vial of clear blond liquid which is a flavour called white peach and he replaces the others in the bag.

The man tilts his head and the brim of his hat covers his hands and he begins to tinker with his pen and refill it while the girl watches, and then thick vapour begins to amass underneath and around him and he comes up and puffs a big peach flavoured cloud from his mouth, then he drops the empty plastic vial on the floor and holds the pen between his teeth.

The girl stands behind the man and waits and watches him with his pen, then she speaks to him in Arabic, and she says, 'They will come back.'

The man turns and looks at her and pulls and blows another puff of candied vapour. The girl looks at him and tastes the peach on the air when it reaches her, then she raises her eyebrows and again speaks with a kind of palled and pushful inflection, and she says, 'The Ali Babas will come back.'

The man looks at her and frowns. Then he tokes and looks back at the horizon and thinks about the Western film *Shane*. He thinks about the beginning of that film where the boy little Joe Starrett, who is a similar age to this girl, looks out into the wilderness from behind a bush outside his farm with a long single shot rifle and pretends to shoot some kind of deer. When he takes aim both him and the deer see Shane who arrives on the horizon, and the boy runs from the bush to the farmhouse where his father is chopping a tree stump and tells his father that somebody's coming. And the father stops and looks up and tells little Joe to let them come, and then continues to chop the stump.

The man turns and looks at the girl and speaks English, and like the father from Shane he says, 'Well let them come.' The girl frowns, and he frowns too because although that father who is big Joe Starrett is brave and of good virtue, he disagrees with Shane at the end of that film and even fights with him and gets punched out. And the man thinks about Shane as a hero and how he helps that family the Starretts and how he helps the boy little Joe in the end and teaches him good lessons like how there's no going back from a killing.

And he thinks about how Shane is both the most dangerous and the safest man to have around because it's clear that he can handle himself in both a fist fight and a gun fight. And then he thinks about how once Shane is tied to that family he is loyal to the end, and how he sacrifices himself for them and for little Joe in particular.

Then Hosti moans and the man remembers the meal Shane has with the Starretts after he arrives at their farm, and he looks at the house and then back at the girl who is still frowning and he speaks English and says, 'Have you got anything to eat?' But the girl just keeps frowning so he gestures at the house and puts a hand to his mouth and chews the air and then pretends to swallow and rubs circles around his stomach with his hand, and then the girl understands and nods her head, and the man takes his camel by its rope and double clicks at it with his mouth. And together they walk back to the house and the man takes his luggage and saddle down from the camel and walks them inside, and then he takes his rucksack and the girl follows him into the kitchen.

The kitchen has a concrete floor and the walls are tiled and grimy in white. There's a tube light in the corner and no windows so the man pulls a cord to turn it on and then sees three open shelves with all sorts of canned meats and fruits, and packaged spices and a bag of rice and a bag of lentils, and there's a fridge and a stove and a sink and some pots.

And on the side is a door which leads to a small bathroom also tiled in white, with a bath and a sink and a toilet which is a porcelain hole in the floor. The man walks into it and sees that there's a large bucket full of stagnant water and washed clothes, and as he is looking at the bucket the girl speaks in Arabic behind him, and she says, 'Sorry I didn't empty that.' The man looks back at her and then puts down his rucksack and picks up the bucket and takes it outside and empties the water, and he thinks that he saw a clothes horse somewhere but can't remember where so he leaves the washing to dry outside on a windowsill, and then he rinses and refills the bucket in the kitchen and leaves it outside for Hosti to drink from. Then he returns to the kitchen and empties his rucksack of Coca Cola and puts all the bottles in the fridge.

Then he arranges some of the pots and looks through the food in the shelf and his stomach begins to make noises. He takes down the bag of rice and a green tin with a picture of a lamb on it that says 'Curry Lamb' and holding them side by side he thinks of making something like a dolma which he knows will be nothing like a dolma, and he takes off his hat and jacket and he starts to cook the rice.

The girl watches him and then joins in to help, and when the rice is nearly cooked and they start to heat the lamb it spits and spoils the white shirt of the man so he tuts and untucks it, and then he remembers where he saw the empty clothes horse and that it was in the second bedroom where there's still a human shape laid out on the bed. He looks at the girl who lifts the heavy pot from the stove. She can barely lift it since she is so small, and he watches her upturn it from the pot onto a plate and then thinks that he should bury the body from upstairs in some way. Then the food is served, and the man takes two cokes from the fridge which are now cool and sits with the girl and together they eat, and the man decides to stay there that night and in the morning to tend to the human shape for the girl.

That night the girl sleeps upstairs in the first bedroom and the man prepares to sleep downstairs on his mattress on the floor in the front room. After the girl has gone to bed the man takes new water outside for Hosti and brings the dry washing in from the windowsill, and then he spends some time at the framed photograph of the family. He deduces that the baby is the girl and that the human shape upstairs must be the body of the older woman, because the men in the photograph are all gone and this he knows because none of the washing includes clothes for men.

The next morning the man rises before dawn and acknowledges those habits which remain of his early life which are to wash himself and to roll out his mat and to pray. When the girl comes downstairs to see the man he goes upstairs and the girl follows, and she waits outside the second bedroom where the human shape lies while the man enters in silence. He comes back out with his vape pen in his mouth as before and the white wrapped body cradled in his arms. He takes it downstairs and then outside and he lays it over the back of his camel. Together the man and the girl walk the camel by its rope to the limits of the small town and find an area where the ground is soft. Then, with some pots taken from the kitchen and facing the right way according to a translucent compass shaped like a credit card on a cord from around the man's neck, they dig a hole.

While they dig, the man thinks about the burial and the best way to mark the grave of the old woman and he thinks about the funeral of Stonewall Torrey in *Shane* and the prayer they say, and he thinks about other funerals in other Western films. And then he thinks about the cemetery at the end of the film *The Good, the Bad, and the Ugly* with all its wooden crosses and he feels a yawn somewhere deep inside him that stretches and whispers and he knows that a cross wouldn't be suitable as a grave marker but he doesn't think much more about that and instead he simply decides to mark the grave with a stone, and after the hole is dug the man leaves the girl beside it and goes to find one suitable. Then they lower the body into the hole and the man throws three handfuls of dirt in after it and says a verse that he knows would be apt to say and which comes from that other part of him that is mechanical with its habits, and then they fill in the hole and the man puts the stone on top of the dirt and that marks the grave. And now with the stone there and the body in the ground beneath it the man stands next to the girl and determines that the stone has a sharpened effect on him and does well to underscore the individuality of the life of the person buried there. And he thinks how many lives are implied by all the tombstones and grave markers in the cemetery at the end of *The Good, the Bad, and the Ugly* and it makes him think about the extent of death there and the morbidity of that scene now in a way that he hasn't before. And then he thinks about the amount of death his country has seen over his lifetime and he imagines it as one boundless cemetery like the one in *The Good, the Bad, and the Ugly*, and for a brief moment he is sad and overwhelmed. And then he thinks of another funeral scene from a Western film which is in *The Searchers* where they sing and then John Wayne's character Ethan orders the reverend to stop praying and says that there's no more time for praying, and with that the man turns and starts to walk away.

And on the walk back to the house the man thinks about the other funeral rituals he has known from a time long past, and on one hand he is glad because he knows that with the white sheet the body was correctly embalmed, but on the other he is bothered because it had gone too long without burial. Then he thinks that people in countries that experience so much violence as his should be allowed to adapt their traditions to their circumstances, and he takes his vape pen from his pocket and brings it up and puts the flavour of peach in his mouth.

Later that day the sun returns with full force since the clouds of the previous day have sailed away across the desert to another town perhaps in tow of the men in black and their humvee, and the man decides to make use of the house and the bathtub. He sets his denim outfit to soak in a special wash of cold water and then to dry, and he lays them across the clothes horse which he takes to the roof. And while his denim dries he wears his white boxer shorts and his hat, and with a sheet to cover his shoulders he goes on a walk around the small town and scavenges where there are still doors to be opened and walls to be scavenged within. He leaves the girl sat with Hosti in the shade outside the house with the red metal door, and she and the camel both seem amused enough and there's no trouble.

By the time the sun makes its descent towards the horizon the man has found only a few artefacts of fleeting curiosity and a small bottle of liquor in the small town, but having always abstained from alcohol as mandated by the ideology of his earlier submission none of this means much to him, and when he thinks of taking the bottle anyway the yawn of that morning stretches once more within him, and he burns red in a sweat and smacks his forehead with his hand and tosses it behind a broken wall and it pops.

And before the man returns to the house he stands in the junction as he had the day before and in his sheet he looks out into the desert the way the men in black had gone and he thinks about the film *Shane* again. And he thinks about the lessons Shane gets to leave with little Joe Starrett, and he thinks about the girl back at the house. And he thinks to himself that before he leaves he should show the girl the film *Shane* because there are some good lessons in that film and some good values that she could get to know if she sees it, and that those lessons and values could help her to get along when he leaves. And also he thinks that at the moment he leaves the last few days spent between himself and the girl might then come to have been like the time spent between Shane and the Starrett family in the film and that he might at that point in fact have been like a kind of Shane himself in relation to the girl, and then he turns and walks back to the house.

* * *

THE MUSLIM COWBOY

That evening the man washes in the bath and then prays, and then he tends to his camel and collects his dry clothes from the roof. He doesn't know what the girl is doing with her time until she comes downstairs to help him prepare a meal of rice with lentils and meat from a green tin that says 'Curry Chicken' with a picture of a brown chicken and a red rooster on it.

They serve the meal and eat in silence, then they sit together in the front room and the man brings through two cold bottles of coke from the fridge and sets them on the floor by the mattresses and the cushions and the kentia palm. He brings his portable disc player from his rucksack along with two handfuls of thin plastic sleeves and riffles through them until he finds *Shane*, then he opens the player and puts *Shane* in and closes it and it whirrs and hums. The girl sits and drinks the coke and watches the film up close, and the man takes his coke to the corner of the room next to the electric heater where his bed from the previous night is laid out, and he vapes and watches the girl and the film from there. From the beginning of the film the girl recognises a landscape not unlike her own, and every so often she turns and looks at the man, and he in turn blows vapour and lets his eyes leave the screen and meet hers in acknowledgement. And after those moments she turns back and watches ponderously the horses and carts and the saloon doors swing in the film.

And he watches as she marvels at the outfits in the dance scene and listens intently to the music in monophone from the small speakers on the player. And she concentrates hard on those scenes that have long conversations in English between the characters, and during one of those scenes the man rises and brings them each another coke and calls it a sody pop like Shane does in the film, and during another of those scenes the girl stands and runs to take the hat of the man from the kitchen where it had been left and puts it oversized on her head and raises her eyebrows at him and then sits back down giggling. And she jumps and then watches with a frown when the antagonist Ryker's gunslinger Wilson shoots Stonewall Torrey dead, and then later she watches the climactic gun fight at the end with a wince and through her fingers.

The man looks as she watches the final scenes of the film with tired eyes, and then comes the last exchange between Shane and little Joe Starrett and it is tinny as it comes from the small speakers, and Shane says that he's got to be going on, and little Joe asks him why, and Shane says that a man has to be what he is and can't break the mould and that he tried and that it didn't work. And the man vapes and looks at the girl in the room and the film plays on, and Shane tells little Joe to go home to his parents and to grow up to be strong and straight and to take care of them, and then Shane rides away on his horse and Joey runs and shouts after him, and in the room the girl sits up and looks down at the player and the film ends. And eventually she looks up at the man and speaks to him in Arabic, and she says, 'Will you leave like Shane?' And the man sits there in a cloud of vapour and looks at her, and then he nods his head at the player on the floor and he quotes from the film in his drawl, and in English he says, 'I got to be going on.'

The girl looks at him and frowns, and with serenity he blows another cloud of vapour and the girl looks away, and then she takes his cowboy hat off her head and puts it on the floor, and she looks at the player and then at the cowboy hat and then she leaves the room. The man sits in a puff of peach vapour in the silence of the girl's departure which resonates in the room in such a way as to hold it by the neck, and then a tiny light flickers at the centre of his being and rises without warning and turns into a feeling that sweeps and pulls across his chest and from somewhere he knows the feeling but he smothers it and stands with a jump, and then he walks over to the kentia palm to pick up his hat.

The man clears his throat and picks up his hat and puts it on his head, then he puts his vape pen between his teeth and bites on it and scoops up the disc player and snaps it shut on its hinges. As he pushes the player into his rucksack, he makes a plan to leave the town not the next day but the day after, then he takes off his clothes and puts them aside and he sleeps.

The next day the man wakes early in the morning to pray, and he washes himself and bends and speaks words in dry ritual. He then uses the bathroom and waters Hosti the camel, and then he makes coffee and uses a glass cup from the tea set in the front room to drink it. He finds some old pieces of clothing soiled and tightly packed at the bottom of his bag, and over the rest of the morning moves between the rooms of the house washing them in the dark and with the curtains closed. From time to time he hears a noise from upstairs and remembers the girl, but he thinks it better for her to remain occupied and in her own world and at the limits of his awareness until he is gone. The morning continues like that until the man takes his wet clothes to the roof to dry on the clothes horse, and then he hears a noise in the second bedroom.

He stops and turns in his hat with the bundle of clothes damp and cool against his naked chest and he presses an ear against the door. He can hear the girl in the room talking to herself and then pausing and then responding to the silence with more conversation in turn. The man listens and hears the language is Arabic, but he can't make out the words. He thinks what strange behaviour to talk to oneself but reminds himself that she is only a young girl, and he thinks about her family and then remembers that people respond to tragedy in different ways.

Then he thinks about *Shane* and he thinks that maybe he is not like Shane here at all, or at least that the girl is not like little Joe, since when Shane leaves at the end of the film he tells little Joe to go home to his mother and father and to grow up to be strong and straight and to take care of his parents, and this girl for her part hasn't a mother or father left to take care of and so has less of a chance than little Joe to grow by that advice, and then the man hears the girl in conversation with herself again and he thinks of another part from *Shane* where little Joe's mother Marian tells her son not to get to liking Shane too much since he'll be moving on one day and that Joey will be upset if he gets to liking him too much. The man feels that same inkling deep down from before that spreads soon and without warning over his chest until again he is able quickly to swallow it away, and to do that he clears his throat and shakes his head and tilts his hat, and then he goes through the window and up to the roof to hang his clothes out.

THE MUSLIM COWBOY

* * *

That afternoon the man opens another tin of chicken and eats it with rice from the night before, and there's still food left once he has eaten so he leaves it on the stove for the girl. Then he puts his boots on and gives water to Hosti, and while his clothes dry he goes again to walk around the town in the heat but this time in the opposite direction and with a bare chest in his jeans and no boxer shorts which are on the roof, and when he looks back at the house to check that Hosti is in the shade he sees the curtain close over the face of the young girl in the upstairs window.

When he returns in the early evening the girl is sat outside with the camel. The man tips his hat to her as he walks past and goes to the kitchen to count how many cokes are left. There are over a dozen so he takes one for himself and brings one out to the girl and shows her how to share it with the camel, and she does so mildly and then giggles. The man returns to the kitchen and drinks for a long time and then waits for the air to come to his throat, then he looks at the shelves and points at the tins to count them and takes inventory of the other food that remains there too, and he thinks about the girl and wonders where the food came from and how long it has been there and how long it might last her after he leaves, and then he hears the girl scream outside.

He runs and finds her in giggles at Hosti who has spat on the floor next to her, and she looks at the man and smiles and then raises her eyebrows at the camel and holds the next laugh in her throat until the camel spits again, and then the girl squeals and takes a quick step back and the laugh escapes her mouth. The man goes back inside the house and closes the door behind him, and he pushes his hat up to rub his forehead with his hand and soon after that he washes and prays.

That evening the girl reheats the food the man made at lunch and brings a bowl to his mattress in the front room where he lies in clouds with his vape pen. He sits up and nods and takes off his hat and he eats. After he has eaten he lacks even the inclination to return to the roof and collect his dry clothes and pack his belongings, so instead he unpacks his portable disc player and his collection of films and he sits and the girl chooses *Fort Apache* which is an old film by John Ford about the goings on around a US Cavalry post starring John Wayne and Henry Fonda and Shirley Temple, and the man looks at the girl and she is insistent and he puts it on for her.

The girl watches the film deliberately and with low eyebrows and a creased forehead. While the man watches his eyes become heavy so he closes them and listens to the sound from the player, and soon after that he falls asleep. When he wakes up before dawn the food bowls have been tidied away but his disc player is still open on the floor with a sunken pillow and his cowboy hat next to it. The girl is not there and the man thinks that she must have finished the film and then gone upstairs to bed. He is relieved to be able to pack his things and leave without the mess of saying farewell. He thinks that she must feel the same way and decides to leave some coke for her in the fridge as a token of thanks for his stay.

Once he has washed and prayed and rolled his mat and packed his player and the rest of the coke from the fridge he walks quietly up the stairs and along the corridor to the window and he slides it gently open. As he climbs up to the roof, he is surprised at how well acquainted he has become with the place even over such a short space of time. He reaches the top and approaches the clothes horse and begins to lift and fold his washing which has gone rigid overnight but is clean and smells fresh, and he holds two brittle socks up to see if they're a pair and that's when he sees the cloud on the horizon.

He keeps his eyes on the cloud and puts the socks down, and he moves to the rug and lifts the binocular glasses there and brings them to his face. The sun hasn't yet risen so the sky is a twilight blue above him and the horizon is illuminated in impossible orange grey. He looks with deepened vision across the desert and studies the cloud. He sees that it's of dust and derived from a motorcade of some kind, and he can tell that it's moving quickly and headed towards the town.

The man lowers the glasses and keeps his eyes on the cloud, and he thinks about his departure on his camel and the road ahead, and then he thinks about the girl and the house, and he looks down at his feet and sees two triangular firecrackers limp and unburst. And then he thinks about the things he has seen in his life and even worse the things he has heard, and though the morning is still terrible figments start to stir in his head and he sees glittering visions of crying and silence and figures piled nakedly in playgrounds and dust and a hung man burnt and slices there made from his side like a shawarma. And then the sun makes its first appearance of the day in the east.

And when he thinks of the east it makes him think of the west, and he thinks about the heroes of so many of his films who ride horseback towards a setting sun, and he thinks of the difference between those who ride towards a sun that sets versus those who find themselves riding away from a sun that rises. And he thinks of the ways that he has made a life for himself like those of his heroes untied and unattached to any place or person as far as he can manage, but he thinks too of the honour of those heroes and he thinks about their loyalty and then he looks down and he thinks about the bereaved girl.

And he thinks that maybe destiny has guided his fortunes more favourably than he had first thought and that what he had first drawn as a parallel between his departure from the house and the story of *Shane* might here be made into something more noble and of more honour than anything to which he has been previously committed. And he knows that his heroes like Shane would show loyalty to the end, and then he thinks that maybe his own story isn't quite at its end yet since if he had sought to emulate the examples of his heroes like Shane in order to survive until now then perhaps to submit at last to their heroism too might help to deliver him beyond survival unto something even greater like satisfaction or fulfilment, and he decides to take the girl with him there and then, and that he will take her to stay somewhere safe away from the roving of bandits and motorcades, and hunger and harm, and he thinks that thereafter he will feel better to ride into a sunset with a scheme completed than away from a sunrise with a stage barely set, and with that and in earnest his story for himself is ordained.

II

TRUE GRIT

Once back inside, the man dresses in a dark T-shirt with large glittered text on it saying 'Holiday Taste of Freedom' in capital letters, and each word is in a different font and colour of glitter. He leaves his jacket open over it and puts the rest of his clothes to one side and his hat on his head and then he goes back upstairs to wake the girl.

He stops at the door to the bedroom as if tied around the waist with a length of invisible rope pulled suddenly taut, but he looks at his hands and then at the door and then he pushes it open and walks in and over to the side of her bed which is that next to the window. He bends down and looks at the sleeping girl and before he reaches a hand to her shoulder to wake her she opens her eyes and looks at him and in Arabic she says, 'Are you leaving?'

The man nods and the girl looks down and says, 'Okay,' and turns away. With his jaw slack, the man looks behind at the door and then out the window and then at the girl, then he reddens with the reversion of language he must make in order to entreat her and he decides there to speak to her in Arabic, and he says, 'Come with me,' and he feels a weight of dread. And the girl turns back and looks up at him and then raises her eyebrows and says, 'Why?' And the man looks out the window into the road and tries to remember the name the girl had given to the men wearing black a few days prior, and then he remembers and he looks at her and says, 'Ali Babas.'

And the girl gets up and the man leads her downstairs, and she asks if they have to leave now and he replies in Arabic and says that they do, and he begins to push the rest of his dry clothes into his rucksack. The girl runs back up the stairs and the man pulls two folded canvas bags from a separate pocket of his rucksack and goes to the kitchen and fills them with tins from the shelves and the cokes he had left in the fridge for the girl, and he fills a canteen from his bag with water from the tap, and his two large plastic bladders which he hauls outside and sets down next to Hosti who stirs from its sleep and turns to inspect them, and then he goes back to the front room and rolls up one of the thin mattresses for the girl and fastens it side by side with his own through a strap on his rucksack.

Then the girl comes back down the stairs with a backpack of her own coloured in the green of the inside of a fountain, and she is wearing her jeans and a pair of brown sandals and a light top that the man recognises from the pile of washing he had hung out to dry two days before. The man goes outside with everything and saddles his prone camel with its leather straps, and on top of that he fastens his rucksack and the food bags and the water. Hosti moans so the man touches its cheek and then he walks into the main road and looks in the direction of the cloud. By then the day has broken and the cloud of dust has grown and the same figments and visions as before return to the man as he looks and this time he experiences them carried softly in shivers over the back of his neck as fear, and then he turns and walks quickly back to the house.

THE MUSLIM COWBOY

The girl waits next to the camel with her bag over her shoulder and looks up at the man as he steps back into the house. He runs through a final time for anything he might have missed that could become of use and when he is satisfied and turns to leave he sees that the glass cabinet is open and the photograph frame inside lies empty. He thinks that the girl must want the photograph of her family as a souvenir of remembrance and he feels pity for her.

Back outside he brings his camel up and takes it by the rope and leads it to the junction. The girl follows and they walk away from the house and away from the junction and away from the cloud in the direction the humvee had gone those days before. They carry on past the fragmented walls and blackened street signs of the small town and before long they're at its limits with the vast desert and a scant road of dirt in front of them. They step off the edge of the town into the expanse and then they're gone on their way.

They walk through the morning and the man casts glances behind them as they go. The cloud forever looms on the horizon but the town grows smaller and smaller until it sets like a sun and is bequeathed to the realms of memory for both the man and the girl, though likely better committed by one than the other, and then there's nothing else to see from horizon to horizon apart from a few banal solitary palms and a grass of grey dusted shrubs that litter the floor.

The moment the town is gone the girl begins to speak in Arabic and complain that her legs are tired and her backpack is heavy. The man who is used to his own company struggles to listen and immediately winces and almost rues having brought her with him, but he feels the weight of his hat on his head so after having tolerated her protestations for a time he takes her bag and straps it to the camel, and he lifts her to sit up on the saddle which seems to settle her chatter until she begins to complain of discomfort even there. And then he thinks of what he might do with her until the sun starts to make the climb to its full height and the heat of the country comes down like a carpet and shrivels what remains of his good sense entirely.

And covered in sweat as he is and on the road under the hot sun it's not long before he too tires, and he praises God in ritual when he sees the terrain grow hilly far ahead because it gives him an idea as to where they might be, and along with that comes an idea to him of where he might be able to deposit the girl and move on. And soon they ride into a land made of large brown mounds, and traded there are the dusty shrubs and single trees of the desert for nothing but dirt and rocks. And for lunch they stop and sit in the shade of one of the large mounds and eat rings of pineapple from a tin and drink water from the canteen, and Hosti chews on an old shrub pulled earlier that morning and there the three of them rest in the shade.

Once they've eaten the man turns and looks at the girl who is sat next to the camel drawing lines in the dirt with a stone, and he rises and treads over to his bag and takes from it a mobile phone flat and silver with a rose gold stripe across its side. The girl looks up at the man and he takes the phone in both hands and walks up the mound and kneads commands into it with his fingers.

He stands in the sun at the top of the mound and lifts the phone to his ear and waits. Soon he is joined by a voice on the other end of the call and he speaks to it in English, then he walks down the other side of the mound to speak away from the girl even though the language is English and not Arabic and has so little throat or tongue in its recital that the girl wouldn't be able to understand the words even if she could hear them. And like that the man and the voice discuss the girl and between the two of them formulate and confirm for her deliverance a plan.

That afternoon the man and the girl ride one behind the other on top of the camel with the man behind and the girl in front, and she is burrowed under the brim of his hat and between his lank arms which grip the strings of the camel's reins. The sun is still fervid and fierce, so to hide from its heat the girl sits under the man's white sheet which she has draped over herself, and it covers her entirely from her head to her feet and so far that a loose end hangs down by the camel's belly and beneath.

And still the girl complains but the man feels revitalised since his phone call and he thinks with a smile that soon he will be on his way without her and completed of his quest like one of the heroes from his films, and so he will be satisfied or fulfilled. And he feels so well about his good deed and its ease that if he were walking on foot it would be with a spring in his step.

They tread the ancient and wavering brown mounds unobserved and pass no other travellers as they go, and in the middle of the afternoon the girl becomes restless and begins to fidget, and the white sheet gesticulates in lumps and swells until finally it settles and then from underneath it comes her voice with words spoken in Arabic, and she says, 'Where are we going?' The man holds his breath and reaches a hand to the brim of his hat and touches it lightly, then he exhales and responds to her in Arabic, and he says, 'To see Ali.' The girl quickly pulls her head out from under the sheet with her hair tousled and her mouth open in a look of disbelief, and with upwards inflection magnified almost to mania she squeaks, and she says, 'Ali Babas?' And the man tuts and shakes his head and speaks Arabic again and says, 'No, not Ali Babas,' and then, 'Ali.' The girl frowns and her head disappears back under the white sheet, and the man feels her shoulders rest against his stomach. He thinks how small and fragile she is and how little chance she would have to survive on her own without someone to take charge and protect her, then the girl speaks again from under the sheet, and she says, 'Who's Ali?'

The man has grown impatient with her chatter and thinks of the part in *Shane* where big Joe Starrett asks little Joe if he can't ask nothing but questions, and then he replies sharply to her in bursts as if fired from a rifle in rounds, and he says, 'Ali is my friend, I am taking you to stay with him, he will look after you.' The girl grows still against him under the blanket and then curtly she says, 'I thought I was coming with you.' The man thinks again of *Shane* and his other Western films, and freedom and the pull of the frontier, and he says, 'No,' and then, 'It's too dangerous with me.'

There is a long pause, pregnant and deep, and silence other than the soft crunch of gravel beneath Hosti's feet as the camel clods dutifully on until it flops its head and moans almost with a sense of the tension, and then the girl again brings her head out from under the sheet and says, 'But what if I don't like Ali?' The man is impatient then and says, 'You will like him,' and the girl hovers uncertainly before disappearing back under the sheet. The man feels her small against him again and thinks and then says, 'Did you like the films you've seen with me?' And the girl replies quietly from under the sheet in a muffled voice and says, 'Yes.' And the man says, 'Ali is the man who gave me those films and he has many more films you can see, so you will like spending time with him.'

After that the girl stays quiet, and the terrain gradually grows steeper and more alpine where there are more trees and scrubs than on the scorched plains. They ride deep into the afternoon and then stop at the fragment of a wall to rest the camel, and the man judges it a good time for prayer. He tells the girl so and they wash themselves with water from the plastic bladders. The man knows they should pray independently from each other, so the girl prays on one side of the fragment and the man on the other. The girl has no mat, but she faces the proper direction and removes her shoes, and she covers what she should on her body in clothes and her sheet.

They ride on until the sun is slack and has fallen behind the hill of their ascent, and in time the man sees an open concrete ruin some way away from the path. He climbs down from the camel and leaves it with the girl at the road and approaches the ruin guardedly. He finds it suitable as hideout or shelter, so he collects the camel and girl and brings them to it, and he lays out their mattresses and they sit. With the camel prone the man removes their luggage from its back and then brings out his portable stove and cooks for them rice and lentils.

Once they've eaten and washed everything clean the man fills a pot with new water for the camel and then lounges on his patterned mattress with the brim of his hat pulled over his eyes and tokes from his pen. The girl for her part lies on her mattress on her stomach under her sheet with her face propped up on her elbows, and the stove sits between them and they each drink from a coke. At some point the girl looks at the man and says, 'What's your name?'

The man activates his pen and draws heavily on it, and then he looks at the girl and says, 'I don't have a name.' The girl raises her eyebrows with her hands on her cheeks and then bold with her tone replies and says, 'Everyone has a name,' and the man blows his vapour and thinks and then says, 'Not everyone.'

The girl watches the man vape his flavoured mist. Soon the sun is gone and there's not much light in the ruin at all, and then the pair of them are there indistinct and as only shadows or silhouettes. The man raises and gulps his coke, and the girl looks at his denim and his hat and then at the bottles of coke between them, and then she speaks again, and she says, 'Are you American?'

The man chokes at the remark and then swallows and stops, and he looks at her and snorts once and says, 'Yes, I am American.' Then he finishes his coke and pockets his pen. The girl looks at him with eyebrows raised, and bold again and with upwards inflection she says, 'But you pray?' And the man is brief and says, 'Yes, I pray.'

THE MUSLIM COWBOY

The man sits up and twists to pat down his bedding, then he lies back and tilts his hat down to cover his eyes, and the girl looks at him and says, 'Who do you pray for?' And the man at the end of his patience tilts his hat back up and grimly looks at her and is terse and says, 'Enough questions. Go to sleep now.' And he tilts his hat back down and folds his arms as if to settle and to sleep.

The girl lies on her mattress in the dark with her face still propped up on her elbows and thinks, and then she says, 'Don't you want to know my name?' And the man shifts and crosses his legs at the ankles and says, 'No I don't want to know your name.' And then he says, 'Go to sleep.'

The girl looks at his dark outline and thinks again, and then despite the man's instruction she speaks again, and she says, 'My name is Nadia.' And the man is quiet, and then he says, 'Okay.' Then the girl puts her forearms flat on the mattress and brings her head down to rest over them, and she shuffles and rearranges herself for comfort in posture, and then she says, 'And you are the American.' And the man is quiet and still, and then he replies, and he says, 'And I am the American.' And then they sleep.

The next morning the American wakes at sunrise and Nadia is already awake and praying, and he turns his back on her until she is finished and then he rises and does the same. They have breakfast and pack down their camp and then leave, and again they walk ahead of the camel for the first few hours of the morning in order to inure it to its heavy load. Soon Nadia begins complaining again of fatigue and after ignoring her for a while the American finally assents to bring the camel prone, and then they both climb up and for the rest of the morning they ride.

While the hot sun and clear sky are made more bearable by the breeze on the hill, they make slow progress up its long slope until lunchtime when they reach the top and then they stop. Nadia and the American eat a tin of mixed fruit between them, and there's enough grass on the higher land for Hosti the camel to munch on and chew which it does happily in gulps. After lunch they make their way down the other side of the hill into a valley and then over a second smaller hill of rock and mottled grass, and when they come down the other side of that they see a small hamlet comprised of a single dry road and several flat concrete buildings in two rows either side.

When they roll into the hamlet Nadia looks around and says, 'Is this where Ali lives?' and the American says, 'No,' and then, 'I've never been here.' They ride past a pair of young boys wearing dusty sandals and jumpers playing with a glass marble in the dirt, and then past a hole in the floor for a well where two indefinitely shaped women wrapped from head to toe in black sheets pull water and pour it into buckets, and all these look up at them interrupted as they go.

The road of the hamlet branches at various short tangents to meet the doors of its houses, and each house is a one storey concrete box behind a short wall. The colours that make up the row are either grey or brown pastel along with some patches of grass which are saturated brilliantly in green in parts but pale and thinning in others. Some of the buildings have at their forepart elongated concrete peaks which extend from their top and are held there by solid grey columns met at their footing by concrete platforms of the same length underneath, and each of these has a step or two leading up into them from the dirt so they look like brutal porticos or short shallow stoas.

It is before one of these stoas that the American slows his camel to a stop and sends it prone. He climbs down and then lifts Nadia off and puts her on the floor, then he touches the brim of his hat to lift it and looks up at the stoa. There's a faded sign of mint green script in Arabic at the top that says the building is a tea house, and two old men sit side by side in its shade on a bench behind a small round table. Both of the men are dressed in dark robes and have grey beards and both are drinking tea, and one wears a kufiya dressing of black and white as a scarf around his neck and the other wears a dark patterned cap. If they had been in rampant discussion a moment before one wouldn't know since after the American and Nadia's arrival they sit in silence and peer at the American as he leans to stretch his hip and rubs his lower back and then takes the steps up with a careful lunge to come under the cover of the stoa.

The American looks down at the two old men and tips them his hat. To the left of the bench where they're sat is a thin metal door that sways at the hinge, and he can hear the hum of a television programme and chattering voices inside. To the left of the door is a wooden board that holds a triptych of posters laminated in battered plastic. With his hands in his pockets and his thumbs at his belt the American saunters and swings on his hips over to the wall to read the posters.

The central poster displays about fifty passport photo sized head shots of different men in a grid of eight rows and seven columns on a white background bordered with a kind of crocheted pattern, and some of the photos have a big red cross over them like a checklist. At the top of the poster is black text in Arabic script that says, 'These people are wanted for crimes against Iraqi people,' and then at the bottom, 'Do not be afraid to report any information pertaining to these individuals to coalition authorities even though you feel it may be insignificant since you will be protected from those who may wish you harm and you will be rewarded.'

The posters to the left and right of that are dedicated to a single man each of presumably greater importance, and the left has one big picture of a man with a moustache and a claret military beret on a black background with red and white script and the right has three pictures of another man in various outfits over a white background with red and black script. Both posters are otherwise similar and have the word 'Reward' or 'Wanted' at the top, then a large figure in American dollars, a name for the man and his crime, such as 'This man is wanted for murdering innocent women and children', and then more information below that, like place of birth or alias names, and then contact numbers with calling codes for inside or outside the main city and a website address for something called centcom which the American knows means the US Army.

The American looks among the fifty or so portraits on the central poster for the face of the strong man from the humvee in the small town and sure enough he is there in portrait and profile, and he looks for the other men they had seen like the one in the cap and the other in the bond but they aren't to be found and neither is the driver, and he thinks that the posters must be old besides and that perhaps those others aren't as widely known or important. Then he turns and looks back and Nadia is still stood beside Hosti, and the old men on the bench are now looking at her and she is looking at them.

She looks at the American and he makes a gesture that he is going into the building, and she skips up the steps and meets him at the door.

Nadia stands small and shrunken behind one leg of the American who swings open the door and steps into its frame, and when he does the tea house which had been full of noise and chatter falls silent besides the inapposite sound of a commercial for insulation plaster which is playing from a small flat-panel television screen in a high up corner of the room.

The American looks at the room. There are men of various ages and generations scattered around an assembly of wooden benches with seats draped over in rugs poised over tall hookahs that rise from the floor and glasses of tea that sit on small wooden tables which are stained and scraped with age. The men all face the American and look fixedly at him in the silence with their mouths agape to such an extent that the tip and hose of a hookah falls from the mouth of one of the men onto his lap. Then Nadia emerges from behind the denim leg of the American to peep too and many of the men turn to look at her.

At the back of the room is a counter with stacked glasses and saucers and teapots and a number of tall charcoal kettles, and beside that is an opening into a kitchen and a fire oven for bread. On the wall beside the television screen is a cluster of photographed portraits of a family and its individual members in frames, and on another wall is a painted mural of a teapot and glasses. The commercial for plaster stops playing on the television and another for a rock music channel begins, and the American is sorry that he interrupted the former since he can see in places that the plaster in the tea house has come loose of its walls.

A standing man with a moustache and grey shirt and trousers breaks his stare at the American and as host sets a glass of tea on one of the tables. This ends the silence for all the men and the tension relents and the chatter returns to the room, and the man in the grey shirt makes his way and disappears into the kitchen at the back. The American takes a few more steps and Nadia follows, and they find a pair of empty benches with a table in between and lower themselves to sit. Just then, a man in a green and yellow plaid shirt appears from the kitchen with a pile of seeded bread which is stacked on a flat cotton wrapped bowl which he rests on his head and both hands. From behind him manoeuvres the man in the grey shirt and he approaches the bench of Nadia and the American and greets them, and in Arabic he says, 'May I offer you something?'

The American looks at Nadia and she looks back, and then he looks at the man in the grey shirt and replies in English with his drawl, and he says, 'Tea,' and he holds up two fingers and says, 'Two.' And then he looks at Nadia and then at the table and then back to the man in the grey shirt, and he winces and says, 'Please.'

THE MUSLIM COWBOY

The man in the grey shirt looks between Nadia and the American and reiterates the order for himself in Arabic and says, 'Two glasses of tea,' and the American nods, and then the grey shirt man with upwards inflection says, 'Shisha?' And the American shakes his head and pulls up his vape pen and shows it to the man and bites on it, and the grey shirt man turns and hastens to the counter where the tea is prepared. As he does, a chubby young boy in a blue striped T-shirt emerges coyly from the kitchen hauling a tall amber hookah, and the grey shirt man sees him and shakes his head, and the boy turns with the hookah and disappears again into the back.

The American and Nadia sit on their benches and look at the room. There's an old man sat alone with a duckbilled cap and his eyes on a newspaper, three more old men with sticks sat together wearing robes and kufiya dressings of black and white, one of which has a glass eye, a group of three young men in polyester trousers and different shirts and tops smoking shisha from hookahs, and a final group of two middle-aged men in short sleeved shirts with trousers who are also smoking shisha.

The man with the grey shirt returns to Nadia and the American carrying two glasses of dark tea on saucers which he sets down before them and then retreats to the back room. The tea is so thick and dark that it's black of colour and there's almost a centimetre of sugar at the bottom of each glass. The American takes one and holds it up to study the sugar. He hasn't had much to drink besides coke in recent days and with a thought for his adapted palate he acknowledges the visibility of the sugar and wonders how much of it he might expect to see at the bottom of a coke should one ever settle and whether it might amount to the lump in this tea. He decides there's probably more in a coke and then takes a bitter sip from the hot glass and frowns. Nadia takes her glass up too, but she just sits quietly and looks at the floor and sips.

The group of three young men have remained with one eye on the American since his arrival and have spoken at length between themselves about the hat and costume that do so well to furnish his eccentricity given the context of his sitting at a bench in a tea house in a hamlet in rural Iraq. From the middle of the group of young men, one with a sports shirt stands and speaks in Arabic with a trace of menace, and says, 'Who do you think you are?'

At this the old man behind the newspaper looks up, as does the man with the glass eye, while the other patrons enact etiquette as if to suggest that the room hasn't so badly suffered the change in tone that it has. Nadia looks up too, first at the man in the sports shirt and then at the American, but the American pays no attention to the man or his question and takes another sip of his tea and frowns again at the taste. The man stands there and watches the American and waits, but the American gives no response and instead holds his glass up and looks again at the sugar lode and then replaces it on the table and takes a long puff from his vape pen. The sports shirt man's eyes widen, and he speaks again and this time louder, and he says, 'Who do you think you are?' and then more urgently he says, 'I asked you a question,' and at the final word he bends and puts his fist to the table in emphasis.

The remaining patrons there in their anxiety then turn to the standing man, and the man with the grey shirt and the young boy who was carrying the hookah both poke their heads out from the room at the back. Nadia is shrunk on her bench with her tea in her hands and looks in flits between the American and his plaintiff. The American brings his vape pen down from his mouth and blows a mist from it out into the room, then he turns the pen over in his hand and studies it. This fresh display of disregard for the man in the sports shirt is the final straw. He ushers his two friends to rise and stand alongside him and then on the verge of shaking he shouts, and he says, 'Stranger!'

At this the old man with the glass eye breaks his own silence and speaks Arabic quietly but with force and directly to the man in the sports shirt and his friends, and he says, 'That's enough.' The man in the sports shirt and his friends turn to the old man, and with anger in his eyes the man in the sports shirt speaks in reproof, and says, 'Enough?' and then, 'Am I the only one brave enough to speak up against the treachery of this stranger?' And he looks the American up and down.

The American winces and picks up his tea, looking from the corner of his eye at the two groups of men. The old man with the glass eye responds to the man in the sports shirt, and says, 'Stranger or not he is a guest in our town,' then the latter continues, and says, 'I want to know why he is dressed like that,' and then, 'Is he torturing us? Have we not suffered enough, that now our invaders have left we must be reminded of them with the arrival of this man in his costume?'

The American hears little of what the young man actually says and instead thinks that he is glad for the intervention by the old man into something the American had the foresight to have determined as the next in a long line of hostile encounters from young countrymen of his after the subject of his outfit. He was by now used to having withheld the use of Arabic in conversation in deference to English, such was the extent of his application in possession by Americana and things of the old West, and that had in the past made easy work of prior encounters of a similar nature which he had sidestepped in the confusion his behaviour might have compelled in his critics, but at times when his silence only served to further agitate a troublemaker the American had from time to time known the full fury of a beating, and those had been few and far between but had each left their mark, and while the pain of such beatings hadn't outweighed that which had brought him in the direction of his garb, he hadn't enjoyed them and did want to avoid them in frequency if he could.

The old man with the glass eye looks up at the three young men and sighs and shakes his head, then he speaks calmly, and he says, 'Yes we have suffered,' and he gestures to the young men, 'But you are too young to remember that we were suffering long before the invaders came.' The three young men look down on the group of old men, and the sports shirt man laments heavily. The man with the glass eye breathes and then continues, 'And now they have left and still you are angry. What more can I tell you?' And he tilts his head and says, 'What more can you blame them for?'

THE MUSLIM COWBOY

The young man with the sports shirt raises a clenched fist and replies angrily and says 'They're our enemy,' and, 'They came to bring our country together and instead they made it worse,' and the old man says, 'Are you angry then that they arrived in the first place, or that now they're gone?' And he looks up boldly at the young men and is flanked on the bench by his two friends who look up with him. Then he looks down and picks up his tea and speaks curtly, and he says, 'Don't be angry because you wish they were still here.'

The young man stands in his spot and seethes, and he looks around the room and sees all the other patrons with their eyes on him, and the grey shirt man and the chubby boy too. He boils with anger and spits venom in Arabic at the man with the glass eye, and he says, 'You senile wretch, what do you care about our country?' And, 'You will be gone soon,' and then he gestures to his friends and says, 'My generation is prepared to fight even if yours was not!'

At this the pair of middle-aged men stand and turn on the group of young men in defence of the old, and between them they say, 'Sit down you troublemakers,' and, 'You're always causing problems in town, why don't you respect your elders?'

The three young men then hold out their fists and square up to the pair in front of the old men. The man in the grey shirt nudges the chubby boy who disappears into the kitchen, the man in the duckbilled cap brings his newspaper in front his face, Nadia puts her head in her hands, and the American looks on.

One of the young men gestures to the American and says, 'Look at him,' and a middle-aged man says, 'Would you call him a man of sincerity?' And, 'He is more likely a madman stumbled upon some fantasy for himself,' and the young man says, 'He's dressed like a crusader! God have mercy on you for supporting it,' and the middle-aged man says, 'Don't bring God into this!'

And then the sports shirt man swings his fist, and its intended recipient ducks and it strikes one of the old men who has stood to move away from the ruckus and he cries out, and the middle-aged men see this and effervesce in their anger and charge in attack at the young men with punches in turn that meet them in patters, and the grey shirt man rushes over to try and separate the parties but takes a punch to the face in the crossfire and he too is forced into the brawl to retaliate.

And before long the old men are stood and swinging their sticks and Nadia and the American look at each other and wince, and the American quickly tilts back his head to chug down the last of his tea and then takes Nadia to escape, and they crouch and edge sheepishly past the furore to the door and past the man in the duckbilled cap who raises his head above his newspaper for a moment only to dip back down in a panic to avoid being met by a flying glass of hot sugared tea. The American opens the door in a hurry and lets Nadia out and then slips through himself, and he looks back just in time to see the chubby boy return from the kitchen swinging a hookah around over his head like a chain and flail and ululating something like a war cry. The American grimaces but then sees another glass coming through the air at his head and he shows it the door with a slam and hears the glass shatter on the other side with a zing and a bang.

THE MUSLIM COWBOY

The old men on the stoa bench are still there and crane their necks to determine what might have caused the commotion inside when Nadia and the American make their break from the tea house in a scarper. The American lifts Nadia onto Hosti and then comes astride himself. He looks back at the old men and tips them his hat with a gawkish smile and then kicks the camel into puttering hops and they skip the dust up all the way down the road and then over the hill as they go, and then they're away.

They ride in that same trot up and down greener valleys deep into the afternoon until eventually they slow and it is then with the sun on its decline for the day that Nadia speaks, and she says, 'My brothers didn't like Americans either.' They're then on their way up the side of a hill with rocks and greenery on one side and a steep drop down on the other, and Hosti the camel huffs. The American remains silent and then brings out his vape pen and sucks on it prolongedly, then Nadia speaks again as if this time to compel him to a verbal response, and she says, 'Are Americans bad people?'

The American feels a curl of pain at the bottom of his back and leans to give length to his spine. He takes a long drag of his vape pen and exhales, and the vapour is now thin since its tank is empty of liquid. Hosti groans and then spits, and the American puts his pen in his pocket and looks to the sky and then closes his eyes and speaks Arabic, and he says, 'Do you think I am a bad person?'

Nadia hears this and thinks for a moment. She sits on the camel in front of the American, and the camel stays staunch and steadfast on its slog up the side of the hill. Finally she replies and quietly she says, 'No.'

They continue to ride up and over the hill, and the sun goes down and the sky turns dark and the land turns dim and blue in the half light. When they come up the side of the next hill they arrive at a small farm for sheep which comprises a fenced pen with a small flock of the animals and a flat concrete house. The American climbs down from Hosti and walks in front holding its rope as Nadia sits on its hump and dozes holding on to the fur at the base of its neck. They walk alongside the pen and Nadia looks down at the sheep who follow the three of them around the inside edge of the pen as if to greet them. The pen is made from tall grey sticks of thin wood from dry trees pitched in the dry ground and tied with rope, and one corner is covered in a blue plastic hootch under which a few tired sheep lie. The rest of the sheep are bunched in the corner closest to the concrete house and look out after the American and Nadia as they approach its metal front door.

The house has one storey and a stairway at its side leading to a flat roof where two large metal cisterns sit side by side looking over the edge, and when they reach it the American prods Hosti to go prone and then lifts Nadia down. She shivers in the cold and the American brings her the white sheet and she folds it around herself twice, then he knocks on the door and takes a step back. All is quiet besides the soft padding of the sheep in the pen. The American is about to look back the way they've come to see if some cloud like the one he saw from the roof in the small town might be there to envelop them before they're admitted when a commotion comes from the belly of the house and then a voice comes from behind the door and pipes up short and sharp in Arabic, and it says, 'Who is it?'

The American notices then that a tightness is gone from his shoulders, and he smiles and replies in English with his adopted drawl, and he says, 'Open sesame.' There's the sound of a metal bolt which twists with a rasp and is pulled with a screech, and then the door scrapes the dust and swings open in a hurry, and there with a smile stands a fat brown man who looks to be in his thirties. He wheezes and sweats, and holds out his arms and replies with a smile in English, and he says, 'You're here,' and then, 'God has willed it.' And then he coughs and takes a breath which rattles against his throat and he uses it to say, 'I thought you might never arrive!'

Then Nadia in her sheet steps out from behind the leg of the American and the man sees her and stops, and something seems to stir in his brain and then congeal in his eyes until he crouches down and brings the smile back to his face, and he says the Muslim greeting and then continues in Arabic and says, 'Pleased to meet you,' and then with a hand on his big chest he breathes deeply and introduces himself, and he says, 'My name is Ali,' and, 'We have a mutual friend here,' and he smiles up at the American and then looks back at Nadia and says, 'And you are?' And Nadia twists on her heels and tells him her name, and he nods and says, 'Hello Nadia.' Then he holds his breath and makes an effort to stand with his weight, and he looks at the American and smiles at him gently, then he stands aside and invites them both to come in and eat dinner with him.

Nadia looks up at Ali and then at the American who gestures for her to lead the way. She steps past Ali into the house which is dimly lit with a few warm lamps and the American follows. Ali himself comes in behind them and then closes the door on the hilly wilds and their clouds of dust from motorcades and seals them into safety with a screech from his sturdy bolt lock.

The house of Ali is similar inside to that in the small town where Nadia and the American first met. In the first room a dozen flat woven rugs lie out over the concrete floor and thin mattresses with cushions line the walls. There's an electric heater and a low table for tea, but most distinctly there's a full wall of mounted metal shelving that carries a collection of nearly two thousand films on disc. Nadia looks at the collection with wide eyes. The American knows the number to be closer to one thousand nine hundred and five as Ali has often mentioned and not let him forget.

There is also an alcove running off the westmost wall like the adyton at the temple of Solomon, and inside that is a large flat-panel television screen fixed to one wall and a roll of cushions laid out at the foot of the wall opposite with a lit hookah smouldering on the side. Ali makes a gesture for Nadia and the American to sit, and in English he says, 'Sit down and be comfortable,' and then, 'Let's have dinner,' and he exits through a door on the right leading to the kitchen.

Nadia looks at the American who speaks to her in Arabic, and he says, 'Sit down,' and, 'It's safe here.' Then he turns back to the door and says, 'I'll bring our belongings and check on Hosti and Ali will bring dinner,' and Nadia stands there and nods. The American tries the door and then thinks of the lock, and he wrests back the bolt and heads back outside and the door falls closed behind him, and then on her own Nadia removes her shoes and considers the room. She approaches the wall of films and looks over the titles and then looks to her left and moves to the alcove. She brings her head around the corner of it and looks inside, then she creeps in and sits mildly on the roll of cushions minding not to topple the hookah. On the television is a computerised animation which shows a sequence of excerpts from the film *Transformers* under a dramatic score and when it comes to rest there are options to play the movie or select a certain scene, and it lasts for a minute or so and then starts again in a loop. Nadia sits there and watches it three times and during the fourth she looks to the side and notices framed portraits of two men with white beards. She has seen them from pictures in her town and knows that they're the Ayatollahs. Then the front door opens and the American comes in with their luggage and Ali comes in from the kitchen with a platter of rice with lamb and vegetables and bread, and he looks at Nadia and the American both and smiles, and he says, 'Let's eat.'

Over dinner Ali explains that the lamb had been slaughtered and cooked that morning ahead of their arrival which he had been expecting since the American had spoken to him on the phone from the road, and that the vegetables had been picked nearby in the day. Ali speaks English with the American until he sees that Nadia struggles to follow and then he makes the same concession that the American had on the road and changes to Arabic.

He explains to her that he had lived in a big city until the war when his circumstances had changed and that then he had made plans to move and live somewhere more remote, so he had come to this farm where he now raises sheep and subsists on the land. From the milk of his sheep he makes yoghurt which he sells, and from that he makes money to buy films to watch in the evenings which is his first pastime and passion. He explains that that is what forms the root of his relationship with the American, who has been happy to employ Ali as something of an agent in the sourcing of Western films since they first met in a chance encounter some years ago and found that an appreciation for cinema was something they had in common, and at that point Ali turns to the American and tells him of a collection of new films he has acquired and that they might not be to his taste in subject or theme but that they're on high-resolution discs and are like nothing else he has seen, and he explains that he even had to buy new hardware to accommodate them and he reels off a list of titles, and the American says he will see after dinner and they carry on eating.

After dinner they tidy up and while Nadia sits the men take hay to feed Hosti, and when they come back they all look at the high-resolution discs. Then the American lays out his bedding in a corner of the front room, and when Nadia starts on hers Ali takes her and shows her a room which is bare but for a carpet and a bed, and he is bashful in posture and talks to the floor but tells her then that the room can be hers. And he leaves her there and she prays and then lies on the bed, and in the other room she hears the

American and Ali talking in English but she can understand none of it and before long she falls asleep.

The next morning Nadia wakes late and knows she has missed the first prayer because the sun has risen and is shining through the window in her room. She scolds herself and makes up the prayer before dressing, then she moves to the front room and sees that the bed of the American is still there but that neither he nor Ali are anywhere to be seen.

Then the door opens and Ali enters and smiles and speaks loudly in Arabic, and he says, 'Good morning Nadia,' and in his hands are handles and at the ends of those are large metal pails. He winces and bends and sets them on the floor and Nadia sees that they're each full of milk, then Ali rises with considerable effort and wipes his lips and forehead with a napkin from a pocket in his shirt.

He asks Nadia how she slept and her reply is a smile and a nod, and then they stand there looking at each other until Ali clears his throat and asks, 'Do you like yoghurt?' Nadia nods, and Ali gestures to the pails of milk and says, 'Do you want to see how I make yoghurt from the milk of my sheep?' and again Nadia nods. Ali smiles and lifts the pails and leads Nadia to the kitchen, and as they go he says that there are even some drinks you can make with yoghurt including a soda that has yoghurt and mint which is Persian, and he explains to her that his heritage is Persian so he knows a lot about it and that maybe one day they can make that together too, and Nadia listens and then says, 'Okay.'

In the kitchen Ali shows Nadia to the stove and with a match he lights two flames on it. Over one he puts a large pot, then he fills a steel kettle with water and places that over the other, then he talks Nadia through the process of yoghurt making, and he pours the milk from the pails into the pot and stirs it, and when the kettle whistles he hands the stirring to Nadia. And he brings from under a table a large ice box and lifts the lid and pours the hot water into the box and then he places a dozen glass jars in the water to warm them. Then to the pot he adds a jar of yoghurt from his last batch and he tells Nadia that they add the yoghurt so special bacteria called cultures can ferment and form a colony. Then together they bring out the warm jars and pour the mixture into them and replace them in the box, and they pour more boiling water inside and close the box, and finally they wrap it with blankets and rugs and then Ali says, 'Now we must wait until the evening.'

With the work done Ali pours them each a glass of water and explains to Nadia that a friend comes to collect the yoghurt he makes to sell in the market each weekend in the city, and then they sit together at the table in the kitchen. After a while Ali says, 'Our friend tells me you have suffered losses in your family,' and Nadia looks at him for a moment and then she nods and says, 'Yes.' Ali shakes his head and with a sad smile he says, 'This is Iraq,' and, 'Every family has suffered in its own way,' and they look at each other, and then they sit together and are silent for a while. And when Ali speaks again, he says, 'God tests us all. The important thing is how you react to the tests.' And he smiles at Nadia and then says, 'You have to recognise that they're tests and face them,' and then he turns his hand into a fist and shakes it, and he says, 'In Iraq you have to be a warrior.' Nadia looks at Ali and Ali looks at her, and Nadia looks into his eyes with a hard stare and Ali smiles and says, 'I think you are already a warrior,' and then he adds, 'And on top of that you can now make yoghurt,' and he laughs and lifts himself up. He gulps the rest of his water and Nadia does the same, and Ali takes both glasses to the sink and sets them on the side. Then he asks Nadia if she wants to meet the sheep and she nods, and he goes to leave the kitchen and she follows.

They walk through the front room and Ali opens the front door and the sun shines into the house. As Nadia walks past Ali, she thanks him and he says, 'Above all remember this,' and she turns to him and he says, 'When God gives you a test you have two choices,' and he walks outside and shuts the door behind them and he says, 'You can either fight or you can flee from it,' and he walks past Nadia and she follows in his wake, and he says, 'But you must pick one,' and then they see the American knelt beside Hosti, and he is whispering in the ear of the camel and he turns and looks at them and tips them his hat, and they walk past him and nod hello, and then Ali is quiet and says, 'Because either to fight or to flee is better than to freeze.' And he looks down solemnly at Nadia and she looks back, and they come around a corner of the sheep pen to where there's a gate and Ali pulls the latch and it opens and they enter.

There are nine of Ali's sheep and seven are adults and two are children, and Ali explains that he had started with six and gone from there, and each has a black head and a grey coat of wool greased and tousled and flat to its back, and after he has introduced Nadia to them by name the two of them leave the pen and go back to the house to escape the heat from the sun which has reached its highest point. By this time the American is inside and sat on his mattress with his bag on his lap, and he is turning its contents over in search of something. He sees them and smiles and then returns to his search. Nadia is about to go to him but Ali reminds her that it's time for the midday prayer, so they go to their separate rooms and do that instead. After that the American is no longer in the front room so Nadia and Ali eat a snack and then looking around her room Nadia finds a magazine for girls and spends the rest of the day with that, and she sees neither Ali nor the American until later when she is called to help prepare dinner which is a stew with okra and lamb in tomato sauce.

After dinner Ali declares that they should watch a film from his collection, and he says that Nadia should have the privilege of selection in reward for her making yoghurt with him for the first time. Nadia is excited and looks through the shelves and the American sits and looks on, and Ali watches and makes the delicate recommendation that she include the new set of high-resolution discs in her selection of titles for consideration. Eventually she settles on a division of Western films from the shelf and Ali laughs and looks at the American with eyebrows raised, and of those she chooses *True Grit*, an old film about a girl called Mattie Ross who recruits a US Marshal to help her enact revenge on the murderer of her father, and the marshal called Rooster Cogburn is played by John Wayne and the two are joined by a Texas Ranger called LaBoeuf whose name is pronounced LaBeef and he is played by the country music guitarist and singer Glen Campbell who the American keeps on his media player and reveres.

THE MUSLIM COWBOY

When Nadia pulls the film from the shelf the American sits up and Ali winces and says, 'This isn't high-resolution,' and, 'Are you sure?' And Nadia says, 'Yes,' and looks at the American who looks in turn and nods, and Ali sighs and takes the disc from Nadia and then brings it to the alcove and fixes it to his player. Then he turns on the flat-panel television screen and Nadia and the American position themselves on the cushion opposite, and Ali brings a chair for himself and places it at the mouth of the alcove looking in and they begin the film.

And at some point during the first twenty minutes, when John Wayne as Rooster Cogburn first enters the film newly arrived to the town Fort Smith with a number of bandits he has captured, Ali slaps his thigh and sits up and speaks English and says, 'How could I forget...' And he looks at the American and says, 'I have something for you,' then he lifts himself and goes to leave the room and he beckons the American to follow, and the American looks longingly at the film to which he has just become re-endeared but relents and gets up and goes. Nadia sees them and sits up until Ali tells her not to worry and to continue watching the film so she sits back and subsides, and the two men move from the alcove and through the front door to the flat of the farmstead, small as it is beneath the crescent moon and its spreading circle of stars. The air is crisp and they go past Hosti and around the house to a metal shed shut with a bar and a padlock. Ali takes up a ring of keys and moves the bar and opens the shed and goes in, and the American follows.

It is dark and dusty in the shed, and full with tools for farming. Ali moves things around and then ventures to the far end where there's a metal unit of shelves, and he reaches to the top and takes down what seems to be a thin coffer wrapped in a coloured shroud, then he turns to the American and speaks English and says, 'I was reminded of it by the badge on the character's waistcoat.' The American thinks of Rooster Cogburn as a shepherd like Ali but of bandits kicking the last of his flock into the courthouse in Fort Smith, and he sees on his waistcoat that iconic golden badge which is the marshal's star or otherwise that of a county's sheriff, and then Ali hands him the coffer. It is heavy and the American winces, and Ali says, 'Open it,' and then smiles and says, 'I acquired it in a trade and thought of you right away.'

The American looks at him and says, 'What is this?' And then he kneels and sets it on his lap. He removes the shroud which in its unravelling reveals itself to be a US flag of stars and stripes. Underneath is a slim box of blue plastic with a handle and black clasps, and embossed on the front is a single word stylised of a brand logo which says 'Colt'.

The American sits there in tremors and looks at the box and then looks up at Ali who smiles wide and nods. The American puts the flag of stars and stripes around his shoulders and then slowly slides a fluttering hand to each of the clasps and flicks them up with his thumbs, then he pauses and takes a deep breath. He opens the box and laid inside on a black foam insert is a long handgun with a revolving cylinder. It is of black metal with black plastic stocks on the handle, and its chamber is discoloured to a marbled kind of bronze. On its snout is an inscription which reads 'Colt Single Action Forty-Five', and strung to its trigger guard is a label that says 'Sheriff's Model New Frontier Revolver'. In some cutaways from the foam are fat shells of lead for the gun to shoot and a golden star badge with the word 'Sheriff' on it included promotionally as part of its limited edition. The American stares at it in wonder. On the underside of the lid is a plaque to stand for the authenticity of the weapon which he reads, and unknowingly he speaks it out loud in a whisper, and he says, 'Made in America.'

Ali watches with all the satisfaction that giving entails as the American lifts the gun from its bedding and holds it in both hands. He feels its heavy weight, then takes it in his left hand by the chamber and without grace fumbles to position it the proper way by the handle in his right hand with his finger on the trigger. Like that he lifts the gun vertically and brings it closer to study it, and the gun glistens under the light from the moon coming in through the open shed door. Then he holds it out in front of him as if to take aim and he exhales with a shudder. He thinks of all the men in the old American West who carried a six-gun peacemaker like this one, and there's John Wayne and Clint Eastwood and then just about everyone else who has the American's fascination, and so many all told that the room around him begins to spin and he is forced to lower the revolver and pinch the bridge of his nose between his thumb and fore-finger. At that moment Ali speaks up, and he says, 'Yours for the way ahead,' and then he is serious and says, 'For your protection,' and then he smiles and says, 'But following your persona too.'

The American stows the revolver back in its box and closes the clasps and swaddles it back beneath its flag, and he stands and brings it with him as a bundle and then falls into Ali and buries himself under his big frame. Ali laughs and says, 'I knew you'd like it,' and the American looks up and says, 'How can I thank you?' And Ali pats his friend on the back and is solemn and says, 'You thought of me with the adoption of the girl,' and, 'It is I who should thank you,' and the American looks on. Then they move together from the shed and make their way back to the house, and the American stores the box with the gun and badge in his rucksack, and rubbing his hands for the future and full of thrill and fantasy he makes his way back to the alcove to continue with the film. Ali in turn is tired of the picture which hasn't gripped him with its pace as a dated production, and he remembers besides an updated version of the same story by the same title that he has seen recently and that maybe he owns in high definition, so he excuses himself and makes his way to bed.

The American sits with Nadia to see the scene where Rooster and LaBoeuf make an attempt to rid themselves of the girl Mattie when they tell the gatekeeper at the river crossing that she's a runaway and there's a reward for her return to the sheriff. The gatekeeper forbids the girl to use the cable ferry so she swipes at his face with her hat and gallops downstream to ford the river on the back of her submerged horse, and from the cable ferry the men watch her and speak, and Rooster says that she reminds him of himself, and LaBoeuf says that in that case they might not get along. The American looks to the side and sees Nadia, and her eyes flit from the screen to the American and their eyes meet, and then Nadia looks back to the film where

THE MUSLIM COWBOY

Mattie and her horse are on the way up the bank on the opposite side of the river to join her new friends, and then she looks back at the American but his eyes have moved again to the film and he is then entirely lost in it, so she looks back too, and together they watch.

The next morning Nadia wakes late in her room and prays and then moves through to the kitchen. There Ali is stood on the table which he has pushed to the wall to reach a cupboard in a high up corner that Nadia hadn't noticed since her arrival at the farm. Its hatch is open and the head and arms of Ali are buried inside it. There's the sound of a heavy object being dragged across the space inside and Ali emerges with a large container of white moulded plastic. The table creaks and Ali brings the container slowly down from above his head to his waist, then he bends and sets it on the table and steps down onto a chair and from there to the floor.

Ali sees Nadia and happily says the Muslim greeting and she returns it and then he beckons her over, and he puts the container on top of the table and removes its lid which is also of white plastic, and he sets the lid away to the side and then looks inside the container and stops. Nadia moves to him and looks in too, and inside there's a bundle of clothes in pink and green and with flowered patterns and stripes, and there are bottoms and dresses with hearts and apples on and tunics in mauve and brown. Ali lifts a pair of pink fleeced bottoms and holds them up to look at them and then shows them to Nadia. Then he stoops and holds the bottoms at Nadia's waist to hang down the length of her legs, and they fall and linger above her ankles. And Ali stares at the bottoms and then he speaks Arabic as if to himself, and he says, 'I forgot how young she was,' and then he looks at Nadia and says, 'As if she had continued to grow not here but elsewhere.' And then he lifts the bottoms and lays them gently back in the container.

Ali replaces the lid and nudges the white container along the table towards Nadia and says, 'You can have these if you like. They belonged to my daughter, though I didn't realise they may not fit your size.' Then he says, 'She was younger than you are now,' and he smiles sadly at Nadia. Then his eyes widen and he puts a finger in the air, and he climbs back onto the table and reaches again into the cupboard. There's the sound of another large container being dragged across the space, and from inside Ali says, 'Or there's also this box,' and he brings his head out to look at Nadia and says, 'I think you are too small,' and he returns inside to bring down the box and adds, 'But you are welcome to try.'

Ali lowers the second container down and says, 'Besides these will be better served tried by you than in the cupboard,' and he sets the container on the table next to the first and adds, 'And you will grow into everything in time.' Then he brings his napkin from his pocket and wipes his forehead and the back of his neck, and he puts a hand on each of the containers side by side and looks at Nadia and he says, 'My wife and daughter were both taken from me,' and he looks down and says, 'Still I love them so much,' and, 'Each day I still live is for them.' And he pauses and takes a deep breath, and then he pats the containers with his hands and says, 'You are between them both in size, try the clothes. You are a nice girl, if you are to stay here with me then I am happy for you to wear them.'

Nadia looks at Ali and then at the containers on the table and she says, 'Who took your wife and your daughter from you?' And Ali looks at Nadia and exhales mournfully. And he says, 'Bad men,' and then with depth he says, 'Bad men took them from me.' And Nadia looks at him and she says, 'Ali Babas?' And Ali looks at Nadia and raises an eyebrow, and he smiles and says, 'Ali Babas?' and he laughs. And then he says, 'No, not Ali Babas,' and then with gravity and venom, and a kind of depth implying a darkness so inscrutable that Nadia is disturbed by it, he says, 'Haters,' and then from the same dreaded depth and with rancour and sadness he adds, 'They were taken by Haters.'

Then Ali tells Nadia to help him bring the containers to her room, and he lifts the first and she takes the second, and they carry them out of the kitchen into the hall and down the hall to her bedroom. As they pass the door to the front room Nadia looks through and sees the American awake over his mattress collecting his things from around him and bringing them to his rucksack to pack, and Nadia stops and from behind the box she says, 'Are you leaving?' And the American looks at her and says, 'I am.' And then from further down the hall Ali turns and with a boom he says, 'Nonsense.' And, 'You're affordable to me as a burden for one more night at least,' and then he says, 'Leave tomorrow.' And Nadia looks at the American and he looks at her, and then she turns and follows Ali down the hall. And that day she tries on various outfits from the two containers, but Ali was right in saying that she would be between his wife and daughter in size and she finds nothing from either container that fits.

In the evening after praying the three of them eat, and their meal comprises a casserole made from eggplant and tomatoes that Ali and Nadia gathered from Ali's field in the day, along with the stew left over from the night before with bread. Once they have eaten Ali suggests a game played with a ring which the American knows but Nadia doesn't, and Ali says he will explain and then stacks their dishes and goes to the kitchen to wash them and to find a ring for the game.

Nadia sits then with the American and they look at each other, and Nadia says, 'Are you leaving in the morning?' And the American says, 'Yes,' and Nadia says, 'Will I stay here with Ali?' And again the American says, 'Yes.' Nadia looks down at the floor and then says, 'Because it's dangerous with you?' And the American says, 'Yes,' and then he says, 'Is that okay?' Nadia thinks for a moment and then she looks up and nods, and she says, 'He is nice,' and then she says, 'There are no Ali Babas here,' and the American says, 'No,' and then, 'There are no Ali Babas here.'

They sit together quietly for a moment while Ali clatters next door before Nadia looks at the American and says, 'Ali told me his family was taken by Haters.'

The American looks at Nadia and sees in her eyes that she is curious and questioning. He turns to look in the direction of the kitchen to see if Ali is close to his return and then looks back at Nadia, and quietly he says, 'This is Iraq,' and he blinks in a tremor and says, 'Many people have suffered here,' and Nadia looks down and quietly says, 'I know.' Then she looks at him and says, 'Where were his family taken?'

THE MUSLIM COWBOY

And the American looks at her and says, 'His family wasn't taken,' and then, 'His family was murdered.'

Nadia looks at the American flatly and sadly and then down at the floor again, then she shudders and the American looks down too, and they sit together in silence. Then Nadia frowns and looks up at the American and he looks back at her, and with unsteady and wavering inflection she says, 'Are Haters like Ali Babas?' The American holds her look and he frowns too, and then he takes a deep breath and says, 'To some people they can be seen that way,' and Nadia says, 'To who?' And the American thinks for a moment, and then says, 'To those who have been wronged by them,' and then he thinks for a moment longer and he says, 'Sometimes to others,' and Nadia says, 'To which others?'

The frown of the American deepens and he brings his vape pen from his pocket and draws from it with resolve and then blows. He draws again and thinks and holds his breath until finally he speaks, and he says, 'Haters is just a word,' and then he blows away his vapour and says, 'But it's a symptom of a schism in our country,' and he says, 'Haters refers to Sunni people and is said by Shia people, and Sunni people have their word for Shia people and that is Rejectors,' and then he says, 'They all mean it to curse,' and then, 'These are not nice words.'

Nadia looks at the American and thinks, and then she says, 'Why does Ali say it?'

The American looks again behind him to the kitchen, and vaguely there's the cessation of the commotion so quickly he speaks, and he says, 'Ali is Shia and his town was for Shia,' and then he looks at Nadia and says, 'Like your town was,' and then he says, 'Beyond that bias it was a band of Sunni people who came to his town and murdered his family,' and Nadia looks at the American blankly and is sad then, and she says, 'So Ali curses Sunni people,' and the American nods. And then Nadia says, 'But I am Sunni.'

The American looks at Nadia and says, 'No, your town was for Shia.' And Nadia says, 'My town was not always for Shia.' And the American looks fixedly at Nadia, and then Ali returns from the kitchen to play their game.

Ali sits and puts a ring of silver down on the table and looks between the American and Nadia before opening his mouth to question the tone of their partaken stare when the American turns and speaks in Arabic and says, 'We need to teach Nadia the rules of the game,' and Ali smiles and explains that it's usually played with a larger group and teams of people but that they can just as well play it with three. And he tells Nadia and the American to place their hands down and to choose between them one who will hide the ring under their palm, and then he says that in study of their facial expressions he will seek to intuit the hider and if his guess is correct he gets a point to the good and then takes his own turn to hide the ring in the pair, and if he's wrong he surrenders a point and stays the guesser.

They play and Ali reaches a score of three below zero before he correctly calls out the American who had held the ring beyond each reset where Ali had incorrectly chosen Nadia over and over to her great joy and the laughter of the table at the degree of friendly ribbing delivered by the American to Ali at his every wrong pick. Thereafter it is the turn of Nadia who makes her guess correctly, then again Ali, and so on. The time goes nicely for the three of them until eventually they tire of the game and Ali who has the lowest score is declared its loser and it is decided that they end the night there. They observe that the American will be leaving in the morning, and Nadia through tired eyes asks whether or not she might see him before his departure. He replies in the affirmative providing that she is awake before dawn, and with that Nadia rises and says goodnight and goes to her room.

Ali looks at the American and smiles, and the pair of them rise. The American looks at Ali who has taken back his ring and thinks about what Nadia told him while Ali had been in the kitchen, and his stomach turns and his memories of the evening begin to spoil. Ali stands to take the ring back to where he had found it and the American watches his friend toddle away and then looks into the room at his camp bed and his bags which are packed and ready to go beside the metal door. From there his eyes wander to the framed photographs of the Ayatollahs in the alcove and then he looks up to the ceiling, and then he brings his eyes shut and he squeezes the bridge of his nose between his thumb and forefinger and he winces.

Ali returns and sees the American and laughs, and in English he says, 'If you are so tired you should sleep.' The American just looks at Ali who stands there sweating and wheezing, and they look at each other for a while until Ali eventually clears his throat and says, 'Is something wrong?'

The American looks back at the ceiling and thinks, and he thinks that while telling Ali what Nadia told him would ruin his chance to leave her at the farm, equally ruined is the idea that Nadia could stay with Ali as adequate recourse away from the danger he found her in to begin with since Ali's discovery of her secret would be a danger in itself. It's clear to the American that his plan for Nadia has actually come undone, and he reproaches himself for ever having expected to find fulfilment of his errand so easily. He swallows heavily and then looks back coweringly at Ali.

Ali looks at the American and frowns and says, 'What is it?' And he puts his hands on his hips and taps his foot for an answer. The American curses under his breath and thinks that as long as he makes a plan to depart on a morning then of course it could never pertain to his proper end, that is, of riding away into the sunset like Shane or Rooster Cogburn, and for that he can only blame himself. He closes his eyes and slaps a hand to his forehead, and then he thinks about *True Grit*, and how at the end before Rooster rides away into his sunset the girl Mattie offers to have him buried in her family plot, and he thinks how those two were both on their own in their own different ways to begin with but then came together in a partnership and made of it their story, and then he thinks of himself and Nadia, but then he thinks too of the ranger LaBoeuf who also engages himself with Mattie and who before the end of the film is dead as a result. Then Ali clears his throat and raises his eyebrows, and with that the American says, 'Nadia can't stay here.'

Ali looks at the American and is confused and says, 'Does she not like it here?' And the American says, 'She does like it here,' and Ali says, 'Then what?' And the American looks at the floor and suddenly says, 'She is Sunni.'

THE MUSLIM COWBOY

Ali looks at the American and the American looks back. From behind Ali's unmoving face the American sees his spirit sink scandalised to a depth beyond easy reach and the blood run to the top of his head to boil. Ali smiles in a tremor and then speaks, and his voice wavers and he says, 'You said you met her in a Shia town,' and the American says, 'I did but she is Sunni,' and Ali says, 'How do you know?' And the American says, 'She just told me,' and then Ali says, 'Then you were not to know.'

Ali moves himself sadly and slowly across to his alcove and lowers his great frame and then drops back in a ball onto the roll of cushions. He looks into the dark screen of the television and breathes noisily through his dense throat. The American can only see Ali's chest and legs and his face is covered by the partition of the wall, and from behind the wall and in a whine then Ali says, 'Why could you not just say she is Shia?' And then he breathes again and says, 'I felt like her thoughts were nice.' And then the American sees Ali's hands reach up to his face, and Ali utters a low moan and with gravity in his voice he says, 'I would have given her the clothes of my wife and my daughter.'

The American stands and Ali sits in silence and they're there like that for a long time both thinking and sighing, and the room aches and the silence is close and surrounding. Then finally the silence drops and Ali speaks, and in Arabic he says, 'You're right.' And then he says, 'She can't stay here.' He rolls himself forward onto his knees and then brings himself laboriously to his feet, and he sighs, and to the American he says, 'You're not like the rest of us here in Iraq,' and then, 'You are your own case and failed in your own way,' and the American frowns, and Ali says, 'But you know enough to understand the ways in which the rest of us too are failed.' Then Ali looks up sadly and says, 'You are my friend and for that I want to help you.' And then he says, 'But you're right,' and, 'I can't offer help to a Hater girl.'

That night the American sleeps very little, and instead he lies awake in his boxer shorts and thinks about Nadia. And he thinks about Ali and he thinks about Ali Babas, and then he thinks about Haters and Rejectors, and he wonders if there's any safe place left for a young girl like Nadia in their country, torn as it is every way from the bottom to the top and from one side to the other and from generations back into the past to as far into the future as is thinkable with not a fix to anything in sight but only a spiral plunging away into more mess and bias and waste. And he thinks about the last time he had given his country such thought and he frowns and thinks that it's no wonder since sleep is time set aside for the mind to unpack and pet down those thoughts that one's not meant to see, and that he trespassing on its work shouldn't be awake to witness it, and he gets up and puts on his jacket and his hat and he tokes from his pen and fondles the box with the revolver that Ali insists despite all else that he keep, and then he counts backwards from ten thousand until he falls asleep.

In the morning the American wakes early and prays and dresses and then moves quietly to Nadia's room and wakes her. She stirs and sees him and then asks, 'Are you leaving?' And the American says, 'Yes.' And Nadia rubs her eyes and looks into the room, and the American looks at her and says, 'You should come with me,' and Nadia looks and says, 'I thought I was staying here,' and the American says, 'No.'

Nadia is confused but silently assents and rises, and the American tells her that Ali is asleep so they must be quiet and to meet him in the front room, and then he leaves her to be. Nadia dresses and leaves the clothes from Ali in their boxes and collects the things she had brought with her from her old town in her small rucksack, and then she exits the room into the hall.

There Nadia looks at the door to Ali's room which has a glow inside that casts a brush of light onto the dark hall floor and she hears movement in the room and then she feels sad for Ali. She doesn't want to disturb him, but she wonders if he will come out in time to see them go, and then she thinks that in any case the American seems to visit him often and she will be glad to visit him too in the future. Then she moves to the front room to be with the American and they go through the metal door and together they leave the house.

III

THE WILD
BUNCH

The American walks ahead holding Hosti by the rope, and on top of the camel sits Nadia holding on to the strings of its reins. She rocks to and fro with its every lurching step under the hat of the American which she has been wearing since their departure from the farm that morning along with his denim jacket which encloses her and is oversized and broad. They left without incident or sight of Ali, and the American had made the decision to leave the downland heights and ride south but to stay away from bridging points on the river or any towns in the hope of circumventing other travellers or bands on their way, so precarious had he determined such encounters to be since experiencing first hand even his friend Ali's disenchantment after learning of Nadia's pedigree, and in the hope that a new idea for his redistribution of the girl might reveal itself in the vacancy of attention delivered to him by the wading of his booted feet on the road.

When the sun comes up they carry on hidden in the shade of the waning hills, and soon they stop for a late breakfast of bread with a yoghurt dipping sauce the American had taken from Ali's kitchen. It is then that the American realises he has forgotten to recover his remaining bottles of coke from the fridge at the farm and he laments his stupidity, and he and Nadia take water into the canteen from one of the plastic bladders and glumly drink it. They sit for a while but the day goes on at its unabated pace, and soon the sun rushes to its true height and pulls with it the shade of their placement and they're made to mount and continue on their way.

Soon the local relief of their route is made level and they're carried at the mercy of the heat without meaningful shelter of topography, and then in flashes of ire and braisedness each of Nadia and the American feel a desire to be returned to the cooler heights of Ali's farm and the comforts of his hospitality. A morning now away from the farm Nadia begins to think about the sheep and their milk and the yoghurt and the vegetables, and she thinks of Ali in his pen and in his kitchen, and then she speaks out loud to herself but so the American can hear, and she says, 'I like it at Ali's farm,' and the American remains still so Nadia steps further to engage him and says, 'When will we go back to visit?'

The American is now sat behind Nadia on Hosti with the US flag from his box wrapped like a kufiya dressing around his head. He looks down at the top of the cowboy hat in front of him on Nadia's head which bobs and rocks with each step of the camel and he thinks that part of her question might imply a belief that she should be staying and travelling with him permanently. The thought sets a cold sense of panic at the back of his neck, and he says, 'We aren't going back.' The cowboy hat on Nadia's head continues to bob but the mood of it for the American as he sees it is somehow changed, either by his words that hang in the air or by the thick silence that sits on a response from Nadia whose mind in its innocence may only just now have begun to question the grounds for their leaving the farm in the first place. After a short while the bobbing head turns halfway around and Nadia says, 'I thought Ali is your friend?' And the American says, 'He is my friend,' and Nadia thinks and frowns and says, 'So why can't we go back?'

The American sits on the camel and thinks of what to say, and after a long while he sighs, and then he says, 'It is difficult to find a definition for friendship in Iraq,' and Nadia is silent and her head bobs, and the American looks down at her in front of him in that same thick silence as before and again he sighs. And then with a start he says, 'In Iraq it's better not to think about friendship. The most important thing is to survive,' and then he says, 'Friendship is bad for survival,' and, 'To have friends is to be attached, and after two become attached is when they can be split.'

Nadia sits in silence and the American sits with her, and together they rock back and forth on Hosti who spits. The American winces in the heat and puts his hand on the back of his head and then says, 'Do you understand?' And after a while Nadia says, 'Yes,' and the American nods, and then he says, 'Friendships are better ignored so you won't find yourself upset.' And he says, 'I can say that I think Ali is a good man, but I can say that every man is good and every man is also bad, and I only need to survive,' then he says, 'If you want to survive it's best to be alone.'

After a while Nadia asks another question, and she says, 'Does that mean that we can't be friends?' The American frowns and his stomach turns and from behind Nadia he shakes his head and looks up at the sky, and he thinks again and then he says, 'You can be my friend as Ali is my friend,' and Nadia says, 'But you left Ali and you brought me with you,' and the American says, 'Yes because I am yet to deliver you somewhere,' and Nadia says, 'Where will you deliver me?' And the American says, 'I don't yet know.'

The path they now ride is at the edge of a scrubbed plain where the land is once again flat and besides the scrubs it is parched and of rock. The American winces at his conversation with Nadia and thinks about where he might now deliver her since the failure of his first plan. He looks behind and sees the greener hills from which they are returned and he sees them rise and loom under the shadow of the rain clouds that can't reach the flatlands, and he thinks about Ali now left in those hills and about bias and its diagonality. And he thinks of the values impressed on him from his films, and he thinks that by the example of his heroes, regardless of what he has seen in the world, he can't take responsibility for how the people he meets might have found their current state of distress and he can only set out to serve them as they are, that is, met on a level plane at the moment that he as a character might enter their story. Then he turns back around and looks out in front at the land, and he thinks again about his next move for Nadia.

The day takes them further through the scrubbed plain until they stop in the afternoon for a short break where they drink water from a plastic bladder and they wash and they pray. Then Nadia sits and draws patterns in the dust and the American brings a full colour map from his black nylon rucksack to unfold and consult, and he sits with legs crossed and the map on his lap and his back against Hosti vaping a new flavour of lychee and he thinks.

THE MUSLIM COWBOY

By the evening the cowboy hat has returned to the head of the American but Nadia still has his jacket since the air then is cool, and when the sun has made most of its descent they find a circle of dry bushes on a dusty mound between which to camp. They unpack their beds and pray but while tending to Hosti the American looks back and sees reiterated in the dusk of the horizon a cloud of dust like the one he saw from the roof in the small town. He can't tell which way it's coming from or where it's going but it is there writ large and may as well be the same one as then, and he shudders and decides that to stop and camp would be unsafe. He tells Nadia to help him pack and that they must continue on their way, and she groans but does, and while they pack he thinks that the cloud should have loomed for him even over their time spent in what he thought had been safety at Ali's, and then he thinks about what the threat of its terrible reassertion and reappearance means for his quest.

And he knows in that moment that Nadia won't ever be safe as long as she stays in Iraq. And as soon as he knows that his plan for her inclines in his mind to meet its next iteration, and that's when he sees it new and improved for the first time and in its most raw form and the rest of it unravels from there.

The next few days for them on the plain are set by a template of travel and prayer with pauses for various manners of thought and arrangement by map or by instinct, and spent at temporary encampments between bushes or solitary trees, or nested within sanded concrete shells left to dry in the desert some time prior and retrieved and made fit for a night and a morning with life and with fire. And each step they take on the plain is another step further from their association at Ali's farm and a step away from its routine, and a change in tone of their time there from a terminus to something more like when Rooster and Mattie and LeBoeuf in *True Grit* visit Bagby's outpost, that is, a stop on a longer road which is not yet ended but is on the path towards where they're headed, and during those next days Nadia and the American are transitioned away from any point of acclimation they had made at the farm into the wandering groove of the nomad, and they're there moved into a state of travel familiar to the American but entirely new to Nadia who identifies and concedes to it on a level so deep as to be entirely without thinking and almost ancestral in quality.

And it is there that the days are made indeterminate and their attributes begin to surround themselves, and they roll and smudge until their sense of meaning as days is lost and the distance they imply in the space of the desert plain is made vague, and by then the only thing left for Nadia and the American is the act of moving forward, along with maybe the thought that at a time to come once an end has been known the accumulation of their travel might from there be looked back upon and labelled a journey. And somewhere in that open space between thoughts and treaded feet and midnight screenings of films for two over vaped pen and bladdered water the American's plan is made patent for a surer step forward, and at last the pair become oriented towards a goal in earnest.

The plan admits itself to the American one night when dinner is clear and water is poured and he riffles with Nadia through his collection of films in plastic jackets and comes across a film he had been referring to in his mind over the last few days called *The Wild Bunch* by Sam Peckinpah, about a band of outlaws and set on the border between the US and Mexico. After the American's recommendation they play the film, and it is rendered again then to him fully and even with its story reaffirmed since the pair have taken to watching their films with captions in Arabic for the benefit of Nadia's understanding, and the film wraps its yarn like kindling around the American's drafted plan while he lies awake that night and the next, and that crawls all over his brain until it ignites and is later stoked and spread in the pages of his map some days later, and then one afternoon on the banks of a large concrete pool where the pair have stopped to wash and refill their bladders with water it is made known to Nadia and there takes the spotlight of discussion and is made fixed.

The pool is the distinguishing feature of a large dam well known to the American as a landmark of calibration between himself and the frontier, and its appearance to them that day he had been happy to regard as an endorsement of his navigational competence for Nadia who had begun to raise her eyebrows at him in condescension over the past few days to tease, not to mention that their arrival to it had come not a moment too soon as their plastic bladders had by then run thin on supply and Hosti the camel had been in great need of a drink.

They skirt the giant pool at a distance and then approach at a point without significance of premises or function, then they disembark and shuffle down a smooth concrete slope that stretches for miles either side around the pool's bank where they relieve Hosti of their bags and saddle and bring it knee deep into the water where it bends and drinks, and then Nadia and the American strip down to their underwear and swim in slaps and paddles. The pool is vast and noiseless, and shimmering and of a colour deep and rich in reflection of the blue sky and the fierce sun, and the water is cool and refreshing and pleasant and cleansing.

When they leave the water they drag themselves dripping up the slope to their luggage, and from their bags they take the soiled clothes of the previous days and bring each piece one by one to be washed in the pool and then laid out to dry in patches on the concrete. Soon Hosti brings itself up onto the slope to lie beside Nadia who for her part has finished rinsing her small wardrobe and now sits in the sun to dry and taps at the water with her toes. The American is stood up to his thighs in the water wearing his boxer shorts and cowboy hat and he washes a thin blue T-shirt with a white ring around the neck and a picture of soccer goalposts and a ball on its chest. He lifts the shirt which is soaked and dark and lets the water run from it, and then he looks at Nadia and says, 'I know where I will deliver you.'

Nadia stops tapping the water and looks at the American and raises her eyebrows. The American makes as if to splash her and she flinches, and then she says, 'Where?' And the American says, 'It will be like the film *The Wild Bunch*,' and Hosti the camel looks into the distance and Nadia says, 'Which one is *The Wild Bunch*?' And the American says, 'The one with the gang of men.' He wrings his T-shirt and water falls in piddles from it to the pool, and Nadia frowns and the American says, 'The Wild Bunch,' and then, 'Their leader is Pike Bishop,' and the name Pike Bishop stands awkwardly apart in the American's drawl, unglottal as it is having come from the surrounding Arabic, and the frown on Nadia's brow dissolves in a wave of recollection as she thinks then about that particular film they had seen in which Pike Bishop and his band of old men had been shot down in a big fight with guns at the end and how she had watched most of it on edge and under stress at its cutting which had been sharp and disorienting, and then the American says, 'And they go over the border to Mexico.'

Nadia looks at the American and he drops his shirt to soak again. He waves it under the surface of the pool and looks at Nadia, and she frowns and says, 'We're going to Mexico?' And the American laughs and says, 'No, but over the border,' and he lifts his shirt and lets the water fall again and then he says, 'It's too dangerous for you to remain in Iraq so I'm taking you to Jordan.' Nadia looks down and taps her toes on the water and says, 'Where's Jordan?' And the American throws his T-shirt over his shoulder and looks to the horizon, and with his hands on his hips he speaks, and he says, 'West.'

Nadia looks at her toes and thinks and remembers from the film the scenes that had shown so many adult women in states of undress alongside men which she had watched curiously and with a sense of unease, and then she stands and moves to collect her clothes and folds them and then dresses and sits back down next to Hosti who looks at her and moans. Meanwhile the American finishes in the pool and wades to its bank to lay his T-shirt to dry on the concrete, and then he sits higher up than Nadia on the slope next to the luggage. He rummages in his rucksack for a new vial of liquid flavour for his vape pen and then he begins to fill it with mint.

Nadia strokes the cheek of the camel and looks up across the huge pool to the other side which she can barely see, then without turning around to the American she says, 'Is Jordan far?' And the American fiddling says, 'Yes,' and Nadia says, 'How far?' And the American says, 'Far, but I know how to get there,' and with one eye closed in attention he holds the new vial up to his pen and carefully pours juice between the two, then he brings it close to check the level. Then he looks at Nadia and says, 'Do you remember the scene in *The Wild Bunch* when they hold up the locomotive train on the railway to steal the boxes of weapons from the army?' And Nadia says, 'Yes,' and the American says, 'Our plan will be like that,' and Nadia says, 'We're going to hold up a train?' And the American winces and says, 'Well, no,' and then, 'But we will ride one,' and Nadia thinks and remembers that she has ridden a train before.

She looks down at her toes in the water and a gust of fresh mint floats past her. It disappears in strings across the pool and she watches it go, then she says, 'Where will we take the train from?' And the American says, 'From a city,' and Nadia says, 'Where's the city?' And the American says, 'Further south,' and then, 'Down the river,' and Nadia pulls her toes out to dry. Another gust of mint floats past and then she turns around and looks at the American who is by now laid out flat on his back with his legs arranged in a cross and she says, 'Will you come on the train with me to Jordan?'

THE MUSLIM COWBOY

The American activates his pen and drinks a great draw into the chamber of his head and then breathes it back out dense as a cloud. It billows in spirals and rolls into a great heavy sheet and with it comes a word from his mouth which curtly is there before Nadia as if spelt out in the vapour, and he says, 'No,' and she looks at him stiffly and is short and says, 'Why?' There's a pause and the mint cloud spreads and then scatters, and the American sits up and looks at her, and he says, 'I told you already, to survive it's better to be alone.'

Nadia looks away and broods, then she turns and raises her eyebrows and says, 'What if there's trouble on the train like in the film and I get shot?' And the American says, 'There won't be trouble on the train,' and Nadia says, 'How do you know?' And the American says, 'I said the plan will be like the film, but it won't really be like the film. Not in that way.'

He bites his pen and stands and takes some steps to the plastic bladders and bends to lift them in both hands. Nadia sits there and stews and thinks about *The Wild Bunch*, and then she looks up at the American and with both of her hands on the concrete she says, 'You're right it won't really be like the film,' and the American looks at her and she looks at him, and she says, 'In the film Pike Bishop says that his gang has to stay together and if you can't do that then you're an animal and you're finished,' and then she says, 'So you're right it won't be like the film.'

The American looks at her and then rises with his bladders, and he turns and walks them a hundred feet or so along the rim of the pool for a place to fill them where the water hasn't been soiled.

BRUCE OMAR YATES

* * *

It had become known even to the American, who undertook his travel in isolation, that the old mainline railway of his country, which ran from the north to the centre and from the centre to the south, had been given a new branch line to connect the railway in Jordan which ran the length of that country from the gulf of Aqaba to its border in the east where it could meet the westernmost railhead in central Iraq. The development had been remembered by the American due to the revelation that it had been built by money from China which had made him think of *The Iron Horse*, an old film by John Ford about the first railway between the east and west coasts of the US which he had seen in the film had also been built by the Chinese. The American and Nadia begin to ride south to meet this new railway and leave the river at the dam so they might continue to travel unmet on the road, and then they venture away from the scrubbed plain and into the desert proper to ride under the protection of the magnitude of distance viewable in the flat land that then surrounds them.

And there headed in a direction and aligned with a destination the tone of their journey is light, and they spend much of their time on the way in puffs of mint and later watermelon vapour and with music from the media player docked at the back of the saddle, and for the most part it is American Country and Western music that tells stories in cedar wood and steel of outlaws and trouble, and for some songs the American joins in to sing. And the further they ride the hotter it gets and one of those days it even seems like the sun is upon them with no sky in between and that to fall from the camel to join the baked ground with their feet might set fire to their soles and leave them burnt there and laid in a crisp.

And on another day they're made to tiptoe through a cratered trail buried all over with pressure sensitive bombs, and on another they're made to lean on each other when they're swallowed by a stormy blanket of sand in two columns and made to close their eyes and cover themselves up and hold on to Hosti who closes its own fat eyes in turn and stumbles in doddles and teeters and sways along until they're through, and on another still they take to telling each other the stories from their lives that they each are willing to spill, and in the slightest of increments then they come to be better endeared, and the American takes to calling Nadia baby sister like Rooster in *Turn Grit* takes to calling Mattie Ross.

And on yet another day they meet a wide road of asphalt which gradually bends to align with their route as if to insist that they completely bequeath to it their fate in failure or fortune and then carries them to an old city scorched and abandoned and in rubble like a biscuit of oats, and its streets are all in ruins or dug up and its transmission poles are fallen or stand angled and leaning and the cables of metal knitting set before to brace the concrete of its buildings twist mangled and exposed, and its cars are wrecked and its walls are swept over with rifle fire and graffiti in scrawls that read things in Arabic like, 'We are the soldiers of the Prophet and God willing we are coming,' and, 'Only one God.'

And while it isn't the city to which they're headed for the train, the American looks at it all on edge as they pass through since with it he feels acutely the danger of the dust cloud which lies always somewhere on their horizon and looms over their every step as if it could crash over them like it has over this city at any moment, not least because with their new plan to visit the train they're due surely to meet less badlands as they go and come closer to roads and cities and other people and all told closer to civilisation, and the stakes for the American once again then are raised and a countdown to when they will surely be caught up appears at the back of his head and rolls down through his nervous system to become kicks from his heels to Hosti to hasten their pace so they can be back again isolated in safety and take stock, and with the camel moaning they go on and soon they're away from that place, but it leaves its legacy on their endeavour since the unease it casts in the mind of the American leads him to bring for the first time from his bags the box from Ali, and that is what happens when they stop that same night.

And it is moved far on from there and back at the edge of the desert where it happens, and walking dwarfed between two great rocky mounds they find a small cove within which to camp and which they discern should serve as better shelter from the cold winds of the coming night than somewhere more exposed in the flat of the plain. And after dinner and a screening of *High Plains Drifter* Nadia takes herself sheltered and enshrouded in her white sheet and the American's denim jacket to the back of the cove and to bed while the American sits at its mouth by the fire with Hosti, and after rummaging for a time in his bags by the beast he takes onto his lap the box for the colt.

He unfastens each of its black clasps and raises the lid and it's the first time he has opened the box since having received it in the shed at Ali's farm, and as he was then he is stirred insensate at the sight of the dark revolver and its star badge within. He takes up the badge and pins it to the centre of his T-shirt and then he lifts the revolver in both hands and it shimmers in flashes against the flames that make its surroundings. Like before he brings the weapon awkwardly into his right hand by the handle with his left and then moves his thumb to the hammer on its shoulder, and he strains to pull the hammer back until with a wince on his face it comes to and the cylinder turns with a heavy click. Then bent over and close so he can concentrate he studies it with cross eyes in a squint and furrowed of his brow, and as he has seen happen in so many of his films he picks at an indentation on its rear so the back of the cylinder slides away and one of its empty chambers is exposed, and he exhales in a puff and looks around and then down for the box.

There are six fat shots stuck neatly in cutaways from the foam, and holding the open colt in his right hand the American thinks that with the danger of the frontier and the vulnerability of his charge now is as good a time as any to become armed. He takes a shot and with one eye closed and his tongue between his teeth he fumbles it into the empty chamber, then he cocks his head and loads shots in the other chambers too. When it's full he closes the cylinder with a snap and exhales with a shudder and holds the gun out in front with both hands. He carefully pulls the hammer back with both thumbs until it clicks again and then he brings it slowly down to rest against the gun's body. Then with a rush in the dark he stands to his feet.

He holds the colt out with its full weight in front of him and tilts his head, then with a closed eye he brings it in line with his sight and widens his legs in a stance. His heart drums and he brings a finger to the trigger, then he brings it all around and takes aim at a lonely shrub close by on the floor which becomes instantly his opponent and obstinate in its stillness against his challenge. Quietly in the English of his drawl the American says, 'In this world there's two kinds of people,' then, 'Those with loaded guns and those who dig.' He bears down on the shrub and then with his thumb pulls back on the hammer until once more it clicks and his closed eye tightens, and he says, 'You dig.'

Then there's a pop and a crackle from the fire and the American jumps, and with his focus broken and without wanting to wake Nadia he brings the gun away and lets down the hammer. He collects himself and then walks back and forth around the cove with the colt in one hand and he has a go at spinning it around on his forefinger by the trigger like Shane and so many other proper cowboys, but it makes not even one good rotation so stiffly he comes down and brings it with him and sets it carefully on his lap. He sits with his back against the wall as deeply encumbered as he is but prepared well enough now with his weapon to endure it, and he smiles. And he looks into the fire and listens to its noise and before long he closes his eyes and is asleep.

THE MUSLIM COWBOY

* * *

The day after the American wakes late still leant on the wall and the fire is dead, and Nadia is moved and sat on her knees in her sheet and the American's jacket at the edge of the cove waiting and looking out into the desert. The American stirs and feels the colt sat heavily on his lap and takes it in his hands before he stands, and he thinks that Nadia must already have seen it but pays that no mind and thinks rather that its appearance with him should come to her as further endorsement of his competence, and with no holster he refers to the part in *Shane* where little Joe is taught how to shoot a gun and when Shane says that some people carry their gun in their pants, and so with his head bowed he jams the colt snout down in the front of his jeans with its black handle in a hook over his waistband. He arranges Hosti and sets aside the empty blue box which he leaves on the floor beside the pit of the fire and then he walks in half parade with the camel past Nadia at the mouth of the cove and winks at her and she follows and the three of them move away into the desert.

Sure enough, after a while of walking Nadia sits on top of Hosti and asks the American about the revolver, and she says, 'I didn't know you had a gun,' and the American looks up and behind at her from the desert floor and says, 'All Americans have guns,' and Nadia is quiet. Then she says, 'Aren't guns dangerous?' And the American looks forward and is casual and refers again to *Shane*, and he says, 'A gun is a tool no better nor worse than any other tool,' and, 'A gun's as good or as bad as the man using it,' and Nadia

117

looks down at him. And having seen so many of his films herself and having come to know them to such an extent as to have understood his perennial trick of their incessant citation she refers herself to what Marian Starrett says in reply to Shane then, and she says, 'We'd all be better off if there wasn't a single gun left in the valley, including yours.'

The American looks back and smiles up at her and then finds the colt carried up from the front of his waistband into his hands and he holds it up high, and as if either in exhibition or the fullness of his fantasy he spins the gun violently and cluttering around his forefinger as he tried the night before in the cove and this time he is successful by its rotation but when he catches it to a stop its hammer comes accidentally against the crotch of his thumb and fires a shot off into the air with a great bang. The American ducks and Nadia cries out and Hosti tramps and nods and moans. The bang rings out carried by the wind into the distance and the three of them are there stopped and stunned to their senses. The American dry and drained looks at the colt and sees it smoke, then he lowers it and in sobriety decides to administer it back to his jeans. He makes a note to better understand its mechanisms and modes of good use before bringing it up to be spun again, and he apologises and smiles weakly at Nadia who raises her eyebrows and tries to calm Hosti, and once that is done they walk on.

Early the next morning they come to a path which runs parallel with another great asphalt road like that which had led them to the old and scorched city, and they follow it. It has been long since they have been travelling south by then, and the road bends around and at some point gains steel barriers on either side to keep its traffic uncurving and there are transmission poles and road signs. So close then to the city where the train is, and so civilisation, the American feels stretched as if with a familiar yawn deep inside going from his stomach all the way to his chest and when the first motor car races past to overtake them he is almost overcome by it. He shakes his head and sips from his pen and keeps himself constant as they go, and when Nadia beseeches him he says, 'We're nearly there.'

As they go other roads join their larger one and then more cars roar past them and soon they do so continually, and before long they're at the top of a hill or the lip of a valley with traffic going past them in booms and zooms in both directions and then below them and at the end of the road they see spread across the landscape the length of the city. It is vast with buildings and roads and sprawling and humming with activity in business and population, and the American looks over it all with his hands on his hips and breathless with nerves but also proud at the proficiency of their procession, and he says, 'Here we are.'

And there is Nadia on Hosti beside him and they both look out at the metropolis and see that sure enough there is the railway line that joins the city from the east and leaves it to the west, and the river is there too and brings grass and meets the railway in a cross. And Nadia says, 'Look,' and points at the city's forepart where the asphalt road of their trail meets another and the two intersect in bends to make a shape like a flower, and further on from that at the main entrance to the city is a large gated arch which stands over the road to the extent of its full width where cars and trucks are stopped in queues and being seen to in study by a patrol of men dressed in green overalls, and the American looks and says, 'It's a checkpoint.'

Hosti goes prone and Nadia jumps down and joins the American, and she bites her nails and points at the men in green overalls and then looks at the American and says, 'Are they Ali Babas?' And the American looks and frowns and thinks, and he sees that of the men in green overalls there are those with short sleeves and claret berets and others with long sleeves and without berets, and he looks at Nadia and says, 'There's a distinction here,' and he points at those with short sleeves and claret berets who are mostly behind booths or otherwise checking cars in supervision of the checkpoint, and he says, 'These with berets are from the Iraqi Army, so we should expect them to be more lawful,' then he points to the others without berets who are swaggering and pushing each other around and laughing and seem not to have a task between them to keep in particular, and who look more like a motley crew, and he says, 'And these without berets are a Shia militia with whom the army is in league.' And the American winces and then says, 'These Shia militia can be as bad as Ali Babas,' and Nadia winces too.

And Nadia thinks back to the American's explanation at Ali's farm of Shia people or those who Sunnis curse as Rejectors, and Sunni people in turn who Shias call Haters and the schism between them which is iterated out to so many of the people with religion in their country, and she knows that she herself is Sunni and so should be pitted by that schism against those from the militia below and even against those from the army, and with the thought of having to go past them under scrutiny she sweats. And she looks at the American and says, 'Why does the army work with these militia if they can be as bad as Ali Babas?' And the American thinks and then says, 'Maybe if they didn't have people like that to work with them they wouldn't survive,' and Nadia goes and sits behind Hosti and broods.

The American walks back and forth with his hand on his chin and Nadia watches him and Hosti moans. He thinks of their inevitable confrontation now with the army and militia alongside his earlier hope of trying to circumvent other travellers or bands in order to keep Nadia safe and their story ongoing, and he considers their arrival away from isolation at the gateway to the city with all its vibrant life and discernment and he anticipates with their entry there a reckoning. Then he looks at Nadia sat in his over-sized jacket and with her eyes young and nervous and he thinks about when he met her in the small town and the time they have spent together since then, and he reiterates for himself in that moment his objective to deliver her over the border to Jordan so she can be safe, and to do that he knows that they need to reach the train, and for that in turn he knows that they need to enter the city. And charged then and rallied to proceed he pulls Hosti up and he moves, and Nadia stands flustered and gulps and then follows, and the city is daubed before them and together they make their approach.

* * *

Once Nadia and the American are beyond the flowered inter-section they find the road that stretches finally towards the arched checkpoint is arranged with short blast walls alter-nating over its two lanes so that any vehicles making their approach are compelled to slow and skirt between them in zigzags, and they walk Hosti in bends around each one. The American takes great strides ahead with the camel and Nadia comes behind in skips to keep up, and before long the three of them are stood stopped together at the back of a queue of cars and trucks in attendance of their turn to pass beyond the arch and into the city.

The American covertly takes the colt from the front of his jeans and puts it beneath his waistband and T-shirt at the back so it might not be found, then he brings his sunglasses up so he might see more discreetly and leans out and looks through them at the front of the queue. There's a collection of Iraqi Army soldiers in green overalls with short sleeves and claret berets in parade at the gate or standing alongside sand coloured armoured trucks fixed each with large automatic weapons, and in the demeanour of these the American sees the cavalry recruits with their outposts in so many old Western films like *Fort Apache* and *She Wore A Yellow Ribbon* and *Rio Grande*, and when he sees them he silently gives thanks to Nadia for enabling him to live out something like his fantasy and he breathes out indulgently and shudders.

Under the arch on a kerbed island in the middle of the road is a twice windowed concrete booth containing two costumed officials facing out from either side with one on the right for the American and Nadia's queue coming into the city and the other on the left for the queue beyond the gate leaving it. Pulled up at the window of the queue coming in is a hatchback car with its driver's hand out and upturned and gesturing in conversation with the official in the booth. Soon enough the hand of the official reaches down to the driver's and returns unto it a gleaming card of plastic which the driver takes and which the American recognises as a document of identity, and the American puts his hand on his forehead and admits his oversight since he's in absence of anything equivalent having tossed all he had which may have related to who he might have been before his possession or the war a long time ago, and he sweats and pulls his vape pen from his jeans and inhales with his lips on it deeply.

Nadia meanwhile is leant to look beyond the queue the other way and sees on the outer side of the arch an area beyond the road in the dust which is shaded from the sun and where there is sat a trio of Shia militia in particular, and they're dressed in green overalls without berets but with black kerchiefs at their necks and beards on each of their chins, and with dark rings around their eyes and automatic rifles slung from straps over each of their shoulders. Of these three the two sat on either side are noisily engaged in a sort of savage repartee while the third is sat quietly in the middle as if their magistrate, and tied around the forehead of this quiet third is a narrow strip of fabric as a headband which is silken and dynastic in the bright green of its colour.

Nadia looks up at the American who by now is in a cloud of vapour and with a hand to his hat as if in thought at the negotiation of their entry into the city, and when she looks back at the three militia the one with the green headband is staring straight at her and she in surprise looks away. When she edges to look back a moment later he is still there with his stare, and this time also with a smile on his face, and with that she hears in her head the word Haters and the Sunni blood in her runs red with alarm. Then the look of man in the green headband shifts from Nadia to the American and comes to rest on his cowboy hat, and then his smile darkens and he touches his comrades to interrupt their exchange and they look at him and follow his gaze to Nadia and the American in turn, and with the attention of all three of them Nadia with wide eyes bolts to hide back behind Hosti in the queue.

With a grimace she looks up at the American who has a hand to his chin and his eyes narrowed in thought, and she taps his leg for attention but he tuts and shoos her off. She looks back at the militia and sees that they're now stood looming with their guns and have left the shade of the arch and are on their way towards her. She dips back and tries again for the attention of the American with tugs this time at his T-shirt, and interrupted then he turns to her and says, 'What?' He pulls his T-shirt back and looks at his star badge which has become tilted from Nadia's pulling and he brings his sunglasses off his nose to his forehead and looks at Nadia and says, 'Now look what you've done!' And then another voice pipes up and says, 'I've not seen an American in months, and a sheriff no less. Are you going to arrest someone, sheriff?'

The American looks up and sees the three Shia militia and balks, and Nadia tries to puff herself up in a show of pertness. There's a sinister smile on each of their faces and the one in the middle with the green headband and worst smile looks at the American and speaks again, and he points at the tilted badge on his chest and says, 'Or is it written wrong and says that your name is Sharif?' And then the three of them fall into each other and are nasty with laughter.

Nadia looks up at the American and waits for him to redress the men but he stands there caught off guard and in tremors with his mouth open and brings himself in the end to say nothing and Nadia frowns. He puts away his vape pen and looks down to straighten his badge and as he does the queue moves a place and he takes Hosti by the rope and Nadia by the hand and moves on, and as the three of them go the militia men follow. The American is tense and they crack more jokes with each other tittering and in whispers and then they laugh even more, then the green headband man comes alongside the American again and notes the sunglasses on his forehead, and he says, 'They say that Americans wear sunglasses to see through the clothes of our women,' and the other two men sneer and snicker in agreement, and Nadia stands there and raises her eyebrows but the American for his part quivers and removes the sunglasses to return them to his pocket and Nadia frowns again.

Again the queue moves and they're nearly at the arch, and if the American had been anxious to reach it before he is eager to now, and there the headband man squares up to him with his rifle in both hands and the two of them come nose to nose, and the American sees that the headband man is hot and bad and the headband man whispers and says,

'Maybe you aren't even American,' and he looks down at the American's boots and says, 'Maybe you are Haters.' Then he looks up at the American's hat and says, 'Maybe you are Haters and you only wear the costume of an American,' and Nadia is seized when she hears the word Haters.

Then the headband man tightens in on the American, and Hosti moans and the American closes his eyes, and the headband man says, 'But the costume is incomplete,' and, 'A sheriff should have a revolver,' and then he steps back and speaks louder, and he says, 'Where's your revolver, sheriff?'

The American is clenched then, and thinking of Nadia he drops Hosti's rope and reaches back beneath his T-shirt and touches the colt pressed in his waistband. He looks in darts between the militia and listens to their goads which taken in turns say, 'Show us your revolver,' and, 'Don't you have a revolver?' And his fingers close around the handle of the gun and he strains with his thumb to pull back the hammer as he had practised on the plain, and he looks between Nadia and the militia men and then as the hammer is about to reach its click the last car before them is admitted to the city and they're next in the queue and the American lets down the hammer and brings his hand back to take Hosti's rope and he moves and pulls Nadia along with.

Together the three of them scarper away to the booth and the militia men are left behind and look on, and at the booth a soldier of the army in a claret beret ushers them to the window where the costumed official says the Muslim greeting before looking up and raising an eyebrow at the oddness of the American in his decoration and attendance there with Nadia and the camel, and then the official says,

'Present your documents.' The American looks back at the militia men and then winces and returns to the official and says, 'I have no documents,' and the official looks at him and then turns and gestures to Nadia and says, 'And her?' And the American says, 'She is too young to need documents,' and the official says, 'How old is she?' And Nadia speaks up and says, 'Eleven,' and the official nods and assents since that's true.

Then the official says, 'Where are you from?' And the American says, 'North.' And the official looks at him and the American looks back, and the official sighs and bends down and brings up a sheet of paper with drawn boxes and a set of questions and slips it through an opening in the window onto the counter where there's a ballpoint pen, and he points in succession at the drawn boxes and says, 'Write your full name and town of birth here,' and then he brings to the counter an ink pad for stamping and points at third box, and he says, 'And impress the print of your left thumb here.'

The American stands and teeters at the window then and looks down at the sheet of paper and its boxes, and then he looks at Nadia beside him and she looks back and he boils. Then he turns and looks back again at the Shia militia stood growling behind with their rifles and then at the soldiers of the Iraqi Army with their berets and blank faces and he looks at the costumed official in the booth, and then without warning he looks as if through the official to stare at his own figure reflected in the window of the booth with its hat and its jeans and its badge, and at last there shaken as he is he picks up the ballpoint pen and flatly writes on the sheet in its boxes those formerly unacknowledged things of his birth now dredged and wrest and redrawn, and he presses his left thumb from the ink to the third box and the official takes the paper to read and then hits it with a rubber stamp in ink and pulls away from it a copy and gives that to the American and thereby grants him and Nadia and Hosti entry into the city.

The American lifts Nadia up onto the camel as the three of them walk away from the booth and down the road before them. When they're some way gone the American looks back at the checkpoint and sees the trio of Shia militia still stood there watching, and when he does the one with the green headband puts his hands to his neck and tugs at the black kerchief there and pulls it up and it stretches over his head as a balaclava and rendered there on it in white where his face should be is a skull, and the American sees it and quickly turns back around and then shakes. He holds the copied paper still in his hand and then he looks at that, and he sees signified there in his writing something bygone and once left behind but of him nonetheless, and moreover tied unquestionably now to the contemporary touch of his thumb by its print. He shudders and folds the sheet away into a pocket on the seat of his jeans, and like that they enter the city.

The road of their arrival is wide and lined on either side with date palms and thick concrete blast walls twelve feet in height and tightly packed side by side. The American and Hosti with Nadia on its hump go beneath the canopy of these and walk segment after segment there unknowing as to what kind of suburb might lie outside that quiet channel until they reach a second smaller checkpoint which opens into the city centre like an unvenerated gate of Damascus and where the blast walls are decorated for their drabness with plastic flowers that hang blanched by the sun in bunches. There the American shows his copied paper to another soldier and the three are admitted wholly to enter a neighbourhood of late morning noise and full notice.

In this city are more people than both Nadia and the American have come upon in a long time, and of these are men sat and stood on streets and in doorways and women in sheets with children on the road, and some of them there are riding in hatchback cars or on buses or bikes, or employed on an errand or trade, and all seem either to be coming or going, or buying or selling, or in some other kind of chitter or chatter with one another, and such exchanges, along with the strange looks that inevitably accompany a costume like his in a place like this, are all things there that the American after his habit of seclusion is made to contend with. And on the side of the road are shorter blast walls of three or four feet, and overhead are billboards and banners of red and green and blue and black and they show portraits of the Ayatollahs and other Shia icons, and slogans written in Arabic, and flags of satin hang from rooftops and windows in black for mourning and red for revenge and Nadia for her part looks on all those and quivers and winces in turn.

And the two with their camel notice as they go how dirty and dusty they are compared to the residents of the city, and then over the whole hubbub is sung a sharp cry wailed and wavering and it is a call to prayer, and the American thinks that he hasn't been called in a long time and he is reminded then that God is close. And thinking of God he realises that, even though he has taken time to read and to pray, he has done so in recent memory only in ritual, and he thinks how much he has forgotten of who God is or how much God must have forgotten of him, but then he sees a street sign that asserts the presence of two railway stations. There's one in the east of the city and another in the west, and he orients them in the direction of the west one and says to Nadia, 'This way to the train,' and she and Hosti follow in silence.

They come to another barricade of soldiers and blast walls and another checkpoint, and there again the American is given strange looks but eventually endorsed by his copied paper and let through, and beyond is another neighbourhood of similar bustle as the first and they find that the city is divided like so, in honeycombs of blast walls with soldiers and checkpoints enclosing different neighbourhoods. And the more of the city they see the more they find that every so often there's a street cordoned off with metal fences behind which are burnt out cars and rubble and broken glass, or shopfronts blown out and exposed, and those parts are not unlike the old scorched city of their earlier excursion, but unlike that city this new one alongside such portions of disfigurement shows declarations of the endeavour of life in resumption seen exercised in the happening of its people, that is, apart from one district of larger houses in particular which is empty of life entirely, and when they go through that the American says to Nadia that it must have been a Sunni neighbourhood in the old regime, and at the news of that Nadia frowns.

THE MUSLIM COWBOY

Finally they arrive at an empty square with the west railway station at its head, and it is a flat grey concrete building inset with brick arches of weathered beige. Between the central two of those arches are a pair of signs that say 'West Station' in English and Arabic, and below those are steps to approach glass panels inset with swinging doors to enter inside. Nadia and the American look up at the flat building and then at each other and then they cross the square. At the front the American ushers Hosti prone with a click and lifts Nadia down, then he leaves the two of them to rest outside and he climbs the stairs and enters through the doors.

Inside is a large hall, broad and still and empty of people on the whole, with rows of clerestory windows high on the walls through which shafts of light from the sun slope to sit thick and full of dust. On one side of the hall is a large glass partition before an old lounge with rows of wooden chairs upholstered in leather cushions of dark green, on the other side is an old tea house which is closed away behind a grille of metal shutters, and on the remaining wall in front are two openings to the platforms and trains outside where the station master is stood wearing a dark green uniform with a cap, and a row of dark marble alcoves with glass for ticket booths. Each booth has a sign above it to identify the province of its destination and a counter with a screen in disclosure of its ticket officer, and all of these but one are shut.

The American looks at the booths and sees that the only one left open is selling tickets through the country's westmost province of Anbar which borders Jordan and would be the best route for them to take in alignment with his plan to deliver Nadia to safety and approach fulfilment of an ending for himself. He closes his eyes and breathes deeply to observe his success and then he approaches the window at the open booth.

Behind the screen is a ticket officer with a loosened tie and a moustache. He says the Muslim greeting and the American simply puts his hands on the counter and says, 'I'm here to ride the train.' The ticket officer looks at the American in his hat and then clears his throat and says, 'Where to?' And the American says, 'To Jordan,' and the ticket officer says, 'The train will take you as far as Tarbil. There you'll have to take another train to go to Jordan.' The American frowns and says, 'Where's Tarbil?' And the ticket officer says, 'That's as far west as you can go in Iraq before you reach Jordan,' and the American closes his eyes again and almost convulses in celebration.

The ticket officer looks down and flicks through a pad before him which could be the railway schedule and says, 'You're in luck since this is the only service running,' then he winces and says, 'The others are all suspended.' Then the American opens his eyes and says, 'When does the train leave?' And the ticket officer says, 'There is one departure each day in the afternoon,' and, 'There are five carriages, three for passengers and two for freight,' and the American nods and thinks and then says, 'Today?' And the ticket officer looks over the American to the far wall behind and says, 'Today it leaves in one hour.' And the American turns to follow the look of the ticket officer and sees a large analogue clock high up there on the wall.

Then a young family of three enter the station and they are a father in trousers and a mother in sheets with their infant child and then their luggage in carrier bags. They come awkwardly with their load to stand in line behind the American, and the ticket officer says, 'Well?' And the American turns back and says, 'Well what?' And the ticket officer says, 'Do you want to buy seats on the train?' And the American's eyes widen and he brings his hands in pats over the pockets in his jeans. He realises his second oversight since not having had documents for the check-point and then he thinks about his life in isolation, that is, moneyless for the most part and as a scavenger. And of course he hasn't currency significant enough to buy seats so he reddens and sweats and then winces and swallows, and then he looks up at the ticket officer and smiles and cringes and says, 'No.'

He steps aside for the family behind who take his place at the booth and at the same time a couple of middle-aged men wearing cotton shirts and a group of young army recruits with green overalls and claret berets enter the station, and all of these have bags and cases of luggage and all of them venture to join the queue, and the American glowers and retreats to the hall and moves into the lounge and sits on a chair. Caught again at an impasse and with Nadia waiting innocently for him outside he removes his hat and runs a hand through his flattened hair and then he looks out through the glass partition and he thinks.

He looks at the family at the booth and the father there gives the officer his currency and receives his tickets in return and takes those with his wife and child and luggage to the station master who steps aside and lets them through to the platforms and the train, and then the American looks down and sees his hat on his lap and he remembers another old film.

And it is *3:10 to Yuma* by Delmer Daves which tells of an escort mission where a rancher called Dan Evans agrees to take an outlaw called Ben Wade to a place called Contention and put him on the train so he can be delivered to the jail at Yuma, and the rancher Dan Evans is played by Van Heflin who is also big Joe Starrett in *Shane* and the outlaw Ben Wade is played by Glenn Ford. The American remembers that he and Nadia had seen the film together during their rambling days before and that he had told her then of the parallel that he saw between Evans' escorting of Wade and his escorting of her, and Nadia had said that she wasn't an outlaw and that the American wasn't taking her to jail and the American had exhaled and said, 'Yes but all the same.' And he smiles now and thinks of the end of the film when Evans and Wade reach Contention and Wade's gang is there to free him and they're forced to sneak around the back of the town and jump on the moving train to escape, and with that the American looks up and returns his hat to his head, and then he stands and moves back to the hall.

The American slides across to the closed tea house and there in line with the opening he looks covertly out onto the platform and sees the young family and their luggage being screened by two officers wearing pistols and shirts with a round badge on the sleeve that shows they're from the railway company, and he narrows his eyes in focus and thinks.

Then he glances back at the clock on the wall and he heads determined from the station.

Outside, he takes Hosti by the rope and Nadia by the hand and starts to move them away across the square, and Nadia says, 'Where are we going?' And the American says, 'To Jordan,' and Nadia says, 'But don't we need to take the train from the station?' And the American says, 'There are other ways to take the train.' And Nadia looks at the American and stumbles with the purpose of his pace and Hosti dodders trotting in turn and moans, and then Nadia's eyes widen and she says, 'We're going to chase it and jump on it after it leaves like in *3:10 to Yuma!*' And the American looks at her and bursts with pride, and he says, 'Yes! Yes! Yes!'

They move along the street adjacent to the square the length of the flat grey station until they come to a mesh fence and walk the length of it to look for a place they might be able to all squeeze through. They soon come to a section which is loose and the American holds it up furtively in the dust as they climb under with Hosti in particular all distended. In front of them then is a long empty plot with dirt mounds and scrubs and beyond that a great flat yard on top of which a network of tracks comes issued from the station spread in succession and crossing in junctions under great pylons that might if it were dark have served to flood the whole thing in blazing light.

Further back towards the station is a wide concrete platform with a long flat slab for shelter. Underneath that the shirted officers from the railway company are screening one of the middle-aged men while the young army recruits are helping the father of the young family carry his luggage and there are also other new passengers coming to the platform, and ready there to receive them all is the five carriage train of the American's purpose. The locomotive at the front is painted a rich dark green with thick yellow stripes and a red chest and then has a layer of dust from its service while the three passenger carriages behind are of the same green below but a mint green above and are inset with windows. The furthest remaining two carriages for freight are red and grey respectively but plain and unembellished and not unlike shipping containers.

From behind a dark barrier the American looks out across the network of tracks and in an attempt to determine the route of the train's departure gazes along the set from the active platform to where they become tangled with the rest. The different sets of tracks cross so many times that he has to do this again and again with his tongue between his teeth and one eye closed until he is confident that he has found a stretch along which they might be able to intercept the train before it gathers speed and rolls away entirely. Fortunately at some point along that determined portion of the track there's a group of carriages in disuse sat close by, so the plan for them becomes to hide behind those carriages until the train passes and then to jump onto one of its freight carriages at the back as Dan Evans and Ben Wade had done in *3:10 to Yuma*.

The American tells the plan to Nadia and Hosti and maps it out for them over the terrain with a pointed finger and Nadia nods and Hosti spits, then he brings his red veil up from his pocket and ties it around his face and with a quick look back at the station the three of them hop over the barrier and dart from hiding place to hole and again to hiding place and so on in skips and hops over the great yard of tracks until they reach the row of disused carriages without being seen and they wait.

Hosti grumbles in the heat and the others implore the camel to be quiet and then watch as the remaining passengers board the train from the platform and the shirted officers board too, then the station master closes all the doors and brings a whistle to his lips and blows, and with that the train makes a long sound from its horn and slowly begins to creep forward.

Soon the train gathers pace and the American takes Nadia by the hand and Hosti by the rope and they trot together on tiptoes to the far end of the last disused carriage and press themselves against it so as not to be seen. The American rushes with an eye closed in focus to trace a final line over the track from the train to them and then touches Nadia and Hosti and says, 'Get ready!' And the train rolls faster and the three of them brace themselves and the American looks around the corner and grips them and with wide eyes says, 'Here it comes!' And they're all ready to spring and the train is about to meet them when it hits a junction with another track and is swept away across the yard and the American's jaw drops. And Nadia raises an eyebrow and Hosti moans and the American winces and slaps his forehead and then grabs Nadia and lifts her onto Hosti and then climbs on himself and strikes the camel to rise and says, 'Run!' And the beast throws its head back and moans and then goes and they take off across the yard in chase after the train.

The train makes another loud sound from its horn and rattles on and Hosti with the American and Nadia on its hump sprints and half stumbles over the other tracks in the yard on its tail. The American has one hand on his hat and the other on Nadia and they're more or less in line with the train but it runs away from them still at an angle on its diversion until at last the track straightens and the train locks there in a line and Hosti the camel at full performance manages to catch up and then they're finally alongside it.

And at the camel's top speed there is the grey freight carriage which is the train's last, and the American sees that it has a door on its side with a handle and he implores the camel to drift closer in its sprint to approach it and when it does he reaches his hand out and the handle is locked stiff. And with Hosti streaking still in gasps and spasms of its burning lungs the American thumps the door with his fist twice and cries out and says, 'The carriages are locked!' And Nadia before him for her part raises her eyebrows and cries out too and she says, 'Just our luck!' And the American winces.

And he tries the handle again and it seems like it should turn on a wheel and he tries it each way with all his might to no avail and then he grips it tightly and his seat leaves the saddle so that then Nadia is alone riding Hosti and the next moment he is there held to the door with his feet either side of the handle and tugging at it with the ground rushing beneath him and the train gathering more speed with each passing moment. And with the American's neck about to rupture from the strain of his pull and all his weight on the handle something in the bolt of it cracks and comes loose and the thing starts to turn, and he nearly falls from surprise but manages to hold on and he also grabs on to Hosti so he is between both beast and machine, and he says, 'Yes...'

Then he leans and spins the handle along its full wheel until the door is moved out like a plug from its frame and slides open and he throws himself through it to board the train, and then he turns and Nadia is there alongside him with Hosti galloping below at top force to keep up with its eyes fat and wide and worry on its face and the American kneels down and reaches out to Nadia and she reaches back and somewhere there with the stretch their fingers mingle and then with a gasp they have each other by the hand and the American sweeps her across into the carriage, and then the pair of them turn back for Hosti.

The camel lollops there sweating and spitting and puffing and wheezing and the American and Nadia slap their laps and reach out and shout and incite it to jump, but the loyal beast still running there is burnt out and beat, and the train creeps to the crown of its capacity and the camel with wide eyes starts losing pace with it and bleats. And Nadia brings her hands to her cheeks and cries out and says, 'No!' And the American pulls his veil down and claps and clicks with his lips and speaks English and says, 'Giddy up, Hosti!' And then in Arabic he says, 'You can do it!' And the camel hears and hones its focus and then surges determined and with a burst it makes up ground on the train, and the American reaches out and rallies it forward and the camel comes bumping against the lip of the wide door and prepares with the fat of its hump to jump as if the two aboard could ever have dragged it up, but just then there's a third and final loud sound from the train's terrible horn and the train finds from somewhere within it a third and previously reserved burst and it springs forward with a spurt, and with a lurch then Hosti falls behind and the American and Nadia both cry out and watch as the camel concedes defeat, and it crumbles to a canter and then stumbles and rasps along to a stop under the hot sun, and it recedes swiftly into the distance and is lost then and gone, and Nadia shouts from the train and then collapses and mourns and the American steps back in staggers and broods and looks on.

Later Nadia and the American sit on the floor of the carriage. Nadia has a swollen face and tired eyes from crying, and the American from a longer kind of slow cooked sorrow at the loss of the camel who had forever been his sidekick and companion is blank and simply sucks wholeheartedly and needfully from his pen. The door remains open and the dark sandy landscape of rural Iraq speeds by as they rush on to their destination which remains Nadia's deliverance, and in a moment the American considers then that the entirety of his worldly possessions had been strapped to the saddle on his missing camel's back including his criterion collection of films and he heeds their loss too in turn, and with so much of his life missing and his person so honed as it is and so far astray from its usual wandering path he is reaffirmed in possession and with commitment to his task.

The cargo in the carriage is stacked in wooden crates and covered in carpets with moulded foam, and at some point the American stands and sways and takes some of the carpets down to use for his and Nadia's comfort, and then he slides the door closed and the pair of them settle in the darkness while the wheels rumble below at their backs and the floor shakes and hums. And after being there in silence for some time Nadia says, 'When will we get there?' And the American says, 'I don't know,' and soon after that with their exhaustion and despite the noise and movement in the carriage they sleep.

They both wake to find that all is quiet and still. The American slides the door of the carriage open by a fragment and they see that they're stopped at a small and flat roofed station. Both the American and Nadia reach their heads out one on top of the other and look at the front of the train and see the family from the city get down helped with their luggage by the young army recruits, and then there's a crack and a jolt and the train starts to move and again they're on their way. The American moves back inside to sit and Nadia stays at the door and looks through its opening to watch the family go and then sees the town there slink by. It is rural and littered with walls and trees and there are lights on in some homes, and it is as she remembers her own town used to be at early evening times, and then it loses density and they're back in the desert proper and away from it and it is lost and bygone of them with everything else from before.

Not long after having left that town and with the train still noisy and fast there's all of a sudden a great loud roar that churns and then thunders past the gap in the carriage door, and when it comes Nadia and the American sit up from their shared states of daze and look at each other and then stand and open the door more so they can look for it. One on top of the other again but with the American holding his hat to his head then in the wind they see ahead of them a jeep car rush alongside the train at top speed with a great cloud of sand kicked up in its wake. It is topless and stood in its bed are six men wearing sports shirts and jackets with kufiya dressings wrapped to cover their faces, and each of them has a rifle held up in his hands. One points his rifle to the sky and bursts a round of ammunition there, and Nadia and the American look at each other with wide eyes and open mouths and dart back inside as quick as they can.

And Nadia in fear says, 'Who are they?' And the American frowns and says, 'They aren't wearing black or green overalls, and no claret berets nor green headbands,' and he looks at Nadia and shakes his head as if in disbelief and with no further recourse he says, 'These are truly Ali Babas!' And Nadia says, 'Why are they shooting?' And the American says, 'Not for what they believe like the others,' and then, 'Just to steal!' And Nadia looks down and then with a grimace says, 'So it is like *The Wild Bunch*,' and the American says, 'Yes it is!'

The American holds onto his hat and looks back outside and sees the jeep drift closer to the train. One of the wrapped men jumps and boards one of the passenger carriages with his rifle over his shoulder, then the other wrapped men shout and their rifles come up and there's a burst of fire from the carriage and it's the shirted officers with their pistols and young army recruits with their rifles in defence of the train. The American ducks back inside and says, 'They have so many guns,' and he looks at Nadia and winces, and she looks up in fear and says, 'What do we do?' And the American squeezes the bridge of his nose between his thumb and forefinger and thinks.

THE MUSLIM COWBOY

There is another exchange of rifle fire from both sides and Nadia stomps her feet with worry. The American looks back through the door and sees the jeep rock and its wrapped men wobble but they hold fast and return as they were, and he breathes deeply and thinks again, and he knows that for the train to be taken would be for them in the carriage with cargo to be found, and so in turn for their journey to end. He looks on as the officers and young army recruits on the train take fire and one of them is hit and falls and then the American ducks back inside and sweats and looks around. Then he touches behind him and harks that boon so far unused of his that he took from Ali and in the next instant he burns and swells and brings his whole self around to where the colt is jammed in the back of his jeans. He grabs its handle and pulls it up and it glistens with its blackness and his mind then is full of Shane and Rooster Cogburn and Pike Bishop and all the rest. His eyes go honed and he pulls his veil up over his mouth and nose. He knows he must help the others to stop the Ali Babas, and so he is determined.

He fumbles the colt to position and pulls the hammer back with more balance than he had before on the plain, and he goes to the door and endeavours not to spin it but only to shoot it as well as he can, and like that he looks out and takes aim. Since the colt is heavy he uses both hands and strains to support it and with bent elbows he pokes its tip out from the door, then with one eye closed and his tongue between his teeth he brings it in line with his sight and looks over its snout and sees the jeep moving back and forth in waves with all its wrapped men shouting and shooting, and without further ado or being able to find focus on a target in particular he fires and there's a big bang and a spray of soot which comes up in a cloud and then a great toll as the shot comes off the frame of the car which carries on its charge regardless with its men undeterred.

The American's ears ring and his arms hurt and the thrill of having found to some extent his target rushes up and fills him with fire and fixedness and he exhales with a stammer and then screams with a whoop, and then he looks at Nadia and smiles wide and then pulls the hammer back again on the colt. He newly takes aim and Nadia comes beneath him to look too, and as two more of the wrapped man jump from the jeep to the train the American takes another shot and it comes from the gun with a bang, and of the four remaining wrapped men in the jeep swerving and shooting one of them screams as if shattered at the spine and then tumbles backwards over the lip of the bed of the car and the American surely has made his mark, and his and Nadia's eyes go wide.

The shot wrapped man is carried back by the ground and comes below the American and Nadia at their door in a rush, and Nadia gasps and the American pulls down his veil and blinks and falls back and then crawls to the door and again holds his hat and looks after the fallen man as he is sucked away from the train and lost to the land, and then there's a rattle around him and it is rifle fire against the door frame and he looks in a panic, and the rest of the wrapped men in the jeep are turned and cursing and taking aim to shoot another shower the American's way.

And while those of them who already boarded the train persist on their way against the shirted officers and army recruits firing from behind passenger seats ahead, the driver of the jeep presses its brakes to bring the others back the few carriages required for them to confront the American at closer range, and the American sees the menace in their eyes and panics and dives inside. He tells Nadia to hide and she goes as far as she can between two of the crates there, and the American grabs the door and slides it shut with a slam and then goes to defend Nadia as he can by crouching in front of her and preparing himself with his weapon by pulling its hammer and holding it up. Soon the cowering pair hear the engine of the jeep roar as it brakes and accelerates to keep itself steady for its men to turn the handle and work to burst into the carriage, and as the door starts to slide open there's a great rattle of rifle fire that comes newly from further back along the track and there's a commotion beyond the door and somehow it stays shut.

They hear the jeep thunder into action and head back to the front of the train again as if chased by someone new, and when the American determines that the racket has moved far enough along he stands and brings his gun and slides the door open again and Nadia joins him and the pair of them look out. At the front of the train they see the wrapped men as Ali Babas in the jeep being chased by a motorcade of two sand coloured armoured trucks fixed each with a large automatic weapon, and the trucks are large and fast and they churn at the ground and tear after the jeep with rumbles of combustion and clatters of rifle fire that for the American are tantamount to a bugle call as if they could be the US Cavalry arrived on the scene to save them at the last, and the American and Nadia both look on and say, 'The Iraqi Army!'

The American resets his hammer and they cheer as the wrapped men who had boarded the passenger carriage dive back from its iron coupler to land face down and flailing in the bed of the jeep before they're carried off at a right angle from the railway in retreat and followed close behind by one of the armoured trucks while the other races ahead to the top of the train and flags down its driver to stop. There's a screech from below and a sound from the train's horn as it gradually loses its speed and then finally creeps to a stop, and then the remaining truck also stops and its soldier incumbents step down and board the train to administer over the damage and injuries that may have been sustained. Nadia and the American furtively watch as they go and at some point during the survey Nadia looks at the soldiers and says, 'Wait,' and then, 'If these soldiers are using trucks from the Iraqi Army then why aren't they wearing claret berets?'

And the American's eyes go wide and Nadia gasps as the fact of who the rescuers of the railway really are is writ large in the stepping down from the truck of a soldier in particular who pulls down a balaclava and has a silken green band around his head, and together they exclaim, 'The Shia militia!'

And he is that same savage and scary man who had been their bully at the checkpoint, and again he is flanked by his two companions with their beards and black kerchiefs pulled over their heads as skulled balaclavas, and he is sharp and hostile and saunters by the train and barks orders at the men and seems to be something like a captain there, and then without warning he turns and the American and Nadia both duck back into their carriage to try and stay concealed but when they do the American's hat hangs in the air where they had been and he sweats and snatches it back in but by then there's a dark smile on the green headband man's face and the truth is that the two have already been seen.

Nadia backs away and the American rushes to slide closed the carriage door but as he does a cruel voice calls out and says, 'American, we've seen you.' And then the door is torn open as if almost away from its hinges. And there is the green headband man with his comrades, and the American is small with his colt and tries to engage it anew with its hammer but they show him their rifles and he is befuddled and they all fall about laughing. And the headband man says, 'I knew it,' and, 'You do have a revolver!' And he reaches up and grabs the American by his scruff and in one fluid movement pulls him out of the carriage and throws him to the desert floor. He seizes up the colt and holds it out before him in review, and then without warning he points it down at the American and fires with a bang and the shot sends up dust from between the American's legs and the American shouts and flounders but he hasn't been hit, and the headband man says, 'An amusing weapon,' and, 'Now it's mine,' and he jams it snout down in the front of his belt.

Then he jumps up into the carriage and brings down Nadia and she comes kicking and spitting until with a jerk he forces her to be still and then he strokes her and she shivers and feels sick, and then he looks down at the American and says, 'What else do you have?' And he tells his comrades to search him and they take the American by each of his feet and lift him upside down and hold him there by his ankles, and his veil and T-shirt hang down from his neck and shoulders and the blood runs to his head and they shake him and his hat falls to the ground, and then his vape pen and the copied paper from the checkpoint fall from his pockets and he winces, and the headband man bends and lifts the paper and looks at it and says, 'What's this?' And then he says, 'I hardly believe it!'

More militia men approach having secured and settled the passenger carriages of the train and they all have skull balaclavas too, and they study the American with menace and their dark ringed eyes are red, and the headband man sees and greets them and speaks to them, and he says, 'This man thinks he is American but according to this paper he's nothing of the sort,' and Nadia looks on lured and curious too and the American looks at her and then at the crowd there and winces, and the headband man says, 'Rather he is from Iraq.' And then he looks at the American and says, 'With a name from Iraq and from a town in Iraq.' And then the headband man leaves Nadia with the newly arrived soldiers and approaches the American, and he crouches close to his face and says, 'Introduce yourself,' and, 'Tell us your name and where you're from.'

And the headband man holds the paper before the face of the American and the American closes his eyes and says, 'No,' and the headband man looks at the paper and then back at the American and says, 'Why not?' And he pinches the American's cheeks until he looks and then the American sees the paper before him and sees his writing on it alongside the inked print from his thumb and everything there whispers to him and he shudders and something stretches inside him, and he winces and closes his eyes again and then after a moment he settles and with resolve he opens his eyes and barks out, and upside down there he says, 'I am the American!'

The headband man laughs and stands then and says, 'Still you say American,' and then he looks up and speaks to the gathered militia and he says, 'Such an American this man claims to be, and yet,' and then he says, 'He has no revolver,' and, 'He has lost his hat,' and then he reaches down and lifts the American's cowboy hat and puts it on his own head and the American winces, and he takes the vape pen too and drags long on it and then breathes out a cloud and he says, 'Have it your way, American,' and then he says, 'But we don't like Americans here.' And then he smiles and says, 'I'm inclined now to count you as one of those hold uppers we chased away.'

All the while Nadia has been boiling seeing her friend treated so undeservedly, and for the first time she pipes up then determined in her own way, and she says, 'No!' And, 'Leave him alone!' And then as if curried to climax by the flame of those first words she is filled with fury and she speaks an extra final one with venom which she instantly regrets, and she spits and shouts it out and it is loud, and she says, 'Rejectors!' And then the American says, 'No!'

And the word brings the whole of the militia to look at her and gasp and then the whole desert plain is cast in silence. And the headband man slowly turns with the cowboy hat still on his head and looks at Nadia and puffs gently on the American's pen, and then he walks to her, and the American hangs there and laments and the headband man smiles and is quiet and says, 'What did you say?' And Nadia is sorry and feels deep shame and she says, 'I didn't mean it,' and the headband man says, 'You call us Rejectors?' And Nadia closes her eyes and the headband man says, 'And so hatefully,' and Nadia starts to cry, and then the headband man looks between her and the American and he says, 'There can only be one reason,' and he says, 'You two must be Haters!'

And Nadia says, 'No!' And the headband man says, 'Yes,' and then he clicks his fingers and barks orders at his men to get the train to go on its way and to bring the remaining armoured truck around for their own departure, and the American is dropped and looks up from the dust and Nadia looks at him and says, 'What's happening?'

And the headband man takes her wrung by the wrist and intercepts her question and says, 'We're leaving,' and, 'You're coming with us.' And then he says, 'I'll teach you the meaning of the word Haters and I'll show you how we must be Rejectors,' and the American fizzes from the blood rushing away from his head and he looks up and is weak and says, 'No,' and the headband man tugs on Nadia and smiles and says, 'Yes,' and then he says, 'As for you,' and his smile turns sickly.

And then he talks to his men in arrangement of a plan for the American, and the two who had held him before take him again but this time by his scruff and drag him along with their ragged division barking and booing to the front of the train to send it on its way and it sounds its horn from its nose in three blows and then goes. And then the rabble is left alone with only the track and their truck in the flat of the desert and under direction of the headband man they work sneering and jeering, and they take plastic ties to put the American's hands together in fists and his feet to his wrists so that he is there on his back like a lamb, and they put his vape pen in his mouth so he is stuffed and then take him and place him prostrate on the track at the mercy of the next train. And they tie him there so he is wriggling and stuck and Nadia cries, and the headband man is rough with her and laughs and then tips the cowboy hat to the American and says, 'An appropriate end for an American sheriff or hold upper.'

Then he rallies his men and takes Nadia by the collar of the American's oversized denim jacket and they all board the truck and it bellows and booms, and it bounds into action and loops and then leaves to the east in a cloud of dust, and the American prone and powerless and in all the peril that his position implies cranes his neck to see them go and then closes his eyes and winces and whimpers with fear and is fraught, and he is all alone there then with the sun and the sand and the wind and his worry, and all told everything is lost.

IV

THE
SEARCHERS

The American lies there and the plastic ties are tight enough that they graze and abrade his ankles and arms, and his body is contorted in such a way that he remains there waiting for his end full of strain. He desperately sucks at his vape pen and blows watermelon mists until the evening slips and the sun falls and the sky turns purple and then deep blue and the ground starts to cool, and then his pen runs out of its liquid and rattles and rolls and he spits it away and breathes only the desert air, and even if he had use of his hands to renew it his vials to fill it are gone having been left in the pockets of his jacket that Nadia was taken away wearing, and with nothing else to flow through his head and to fuzzy his mind then he thinks of the girl.

And he thinks of the last word she had left on the episode of their uncoupling and her abduction, and he thinks about Ali and the Shia militia and the schism in his country of Haters and Rejectors and he thinks of Nadia then taken for it as if in terrible libation and he shudders. And he thinks of the cloud from the desert that he had seen in the small town where he first met Nadia which had felt so often apparent and from which he had tried to keep them running since then, and he thinks of it as that same cloud the militia had kicked up once they had taken Nadia and hurtled away and he sees it now having outrun them and taken them over and he thinks of what the militia might do to her, and then he closes his eyes and not for the first time is bounced between visions of burden and bale and wickedness and menace and mess, and then the sun disappears beneath the horizon in the west.

And as it grows steadily darker he sees Nadia stood before him as if in spirit with her eyebrows raised and her young eyes petitioning, and he thinks about when he first met her in the small town and of his circumstances then versus now and where he is and how he has all but strayed from the life he had made for himself as the American since his assumption of responsibility over her and his affiliation with her, and he thinks of his things like his films and his jacket and his hat and his life itself which is now on the line and he thinks of the points at which all of them have been lost, and then with her before him now in apparition and looking at her there as he is he finds himself thinking it possible that those adjudications on his fortune might at those or these moments have been suffered not because of her, but for her.

And the desert plain is dark then and the wind blows with a chill which makes the American shiver in his T-shirt and brings up billows of sand that cover from him a view of the stars, and as time passes he lies there drifting in and out of sleep knowing that at some point when the sun comes up the next day a train will arrive and pass over him and then he'll be dead and from the fear and despair of that in moments he cries.

And at some point during the night or perhaps imagined by the American in a dream the sand blows thicker and faster in a storm and lashes him all over, and it tears at his skin and collects in the crevices of his body taut there as it is, and it goes in his mouth too and then with wide eyes he gags and spits, and he swallows and retches and coughs and then he cries a sorry rheum, and there are clods of it stuck in his chest and other clods that arrive in his stomach and rattle inside and as far as he can he bows and convulses and his stomach rises and falls. And then from under his stomach returns that same stretch he has felt before and it extends over the rest of everything within him like a deep yawn, and then he burns red in a sweat and then the great deep yawn rises to hit its crest in his chest and it comes up and over the other side or out through the top of him and everything there then reaches its peak.

And stretched there in that moment the American is collapsed in on himself, and the wind and the sand and the railway and all else above him grows muffled and blurry and he is taken down into a dark place within where he hears whispers and sees visions, and somewhere deep in that vagueness is the impression of something else and he sees it and it grows and engulfs him and then he knows what it is.

And it's something like the memory of himself before his absorption in his Americanness, the memory of that person from the copied paper at the checkpoint who had existed before his screenings of *Stagecoach* and *The Searchers*, and *A Fistful of Dollars* and *High Plains Drifter* and *Red River* and *Rio Bravo*, and before *Once Upon a Time in the West* and *True Grit* and *The Wild Bunch*, and *The Good, the Bad and the Ugly* and *Shane*, and before his disregard for an old self dropped in favour of a stronger one made new.

And as the American he looks down at that dropped self and sees it there rejected with its grief and fear and he remembers it fully and the reasons for its withdrawal, and then he looks down at it not as the American but as someone else and he notices that he has become isolated and alone there in a kind of limbo between selves like the body of Tamerlane neither able to be received by heaven nor by earth and suspended between the two, and looking at that new self of the American in its fullness from without for the first time he sees the extent of its artificiality and sees that it has been so unsteady since his submission to it at the beginning that it could never have been truly taken in place of the other older self.

And he watches as both selves old and new meet then and make conversation in the void and he comes close to madness as if with double vision but double veiled of his soul, and he wonders which of the two he might at this point be left to die with when all is said and done but observing between them as he is he comes to understand that he will from now on or at least until the train arrives be at once neither and both, and that he is to die there renewed, and not returned to his old grief but forgiven and accepting of it and with his Americanness not held up as a mirror but whole of himself and absorbed and essential.

And then he thinks again about Nadia and he sees her there too, and he is relieved and grateful for that absorption of his American mirror and the clarity it has afforded him as an individual against the confusion in his country since the war, and he is grateful for sacrifice as its first virtue that he knew from *Shane* for encouraging his dedication to Nadia in the first place and then for loyalty that he learnt from *True Grit* and *The Wild Bunch* as the second which helped to uphold his charge because he has at least for a time been found in a land of grief and loss with someone to dote on and someone to be responsible for.

And then he sees a third virtue in his Americanness, and that is truthfulness, and this looms larger on him now than the others and he sees that it runs as a thread through maybe all of the films of his recent possession and yet has until now remained hidden as an unknown unknown in his American mirror due to the nature of what that had been, and along with that discovery comes a reproach for his willingness to ride alone into a sunset since the outset when his story so obviously seems to have been preordained oppositely and for him to have ended up somewhere in ministry with Nadia, and he puts that down to his fear and a misinterpretation of his heroes and he sees now that they ride away alone not because they're untied to person or place or unable to survive alongside others but simply because there are no companions for them and the truth is that he had found for himself a companion in Nadia and that, after all, had truly been that.

And then he comes back to the desert and the wind and the railway and he sees everything new as if finally of colour through the three sided prism of his admitted virtues. And he decides to make a final sacrifice before he should die which is to relinquish the ease of his American mirror and everything material it used to entail in turn so that he might commit himself in his final moments entirely in his loyalty to Nadia with all the grief and fear that might be implied of his true self measured equally in its Arabness and Americanness as it is. And he heaves and his stomach swells and all the sand he had in fact swallowed in the storm comes up through his neck and brings with it pain and blood and he vomits the whole thing out in a mess onto the track before him, and then he coughs and spits and slumps there in a lump.

And when the man who had been the American next opens his eyes the sun is rising and the horizon is illuminated the colour of that same impossible orange grey that so many of his dawns spent as a nomad have shown him, and apprised of or at peace then with himself he looks with deepened vision across the desert to it so he can study its majesty in full one last time. And there despite the reconciliation of his two distinct parts a moment from *Shane* comes to his mind and he smiles, and it's that part where big Joe Starrett is about to leave his wife Marian to go and confront Ryker and his men to accomplish what he must by the end of the film, and on the track there and looking at the sunrise he sees Marian desperate and then Joe Starrett tell her that she's the most honest and finest girl that ever lived and that he couldn't do what he had to do if he hadn't always known that he could trust her, and he thinks about having the same conversation with Nadia. And alone now he finishes the scene, and he speaks to himself, and he says, 'Don't go counting me out,' and, 'I wouldn't have lived as long as I had already if I wasn't pretty tough.'

And the man who had been the American looks at himself there and notices that he doesn't want to die, and not just from fear as before but from his devotion to Nadia and his renewed faith in himself to survive despite everything, and then he starts to struggle. And he wriggles and flails and twists and threshes and turns but nothing he does serves to help, and his wrists and ankles then are torn at and cut, and he knows that the train there runs once a day and that if he can't get free then he will so soon be ended. And he looks for something to cut his ties with or some way to escape but nothing will do, and then the sun rises higher, and the day grows hot and with no hat for his head he is exposed moreover and he sweats and goes red and he burns.

And all along he expects to see his deliverance come fast and fierce without warning on its way west along the track and he tries to see the sun to determine when it might arrive, and forever he is craning his neck to watch yet if it comes so he can be ready when it does, and then at some point he sees it and it moves darkly in a block as a hovering blob that begins steadily to grow and then wobble on the horizon, and then he cries out and struggles even further in earnest until he is at the moment of surrender and then knowing the inevitable he lies silent and closes his eyes and urgently he prays.

But he hears no rumble with the train's approach and then he thinks surely that it should already have been over him, and he strains himself to see and looks again. And then gradually and through the heat's wavering haze he sees what it is that has made its approach and then in an instant he knows that it isn't a train or anything even close and he knows then that he lies there revived or at least delivered with a chance to be saved since the block moving westwards faithful and tired and loyal to the last and lolling in trots and the most lopeful of slopes with its drooping head and its fat and folded eyes and its loaded and saddled hump is Hosti the camel.

The man who had been the American sobs and screams on the track and the camel comes steadily closer until finally it arrives and then he greets it with twists and wriggles as far as he can and the camel stands awkwardly over him and then tramps and moans. And he praises the camel and knows that it must have followed him and Nadia once they had outrun and left it on the track behind their train, and he thinks of it alone and dogged in its trudgery that last day and night to come after them and not to give up and he marvels at the beast and pays heed to it and cries.

And after their meeting the man remembers the circumstance of his peril and strains to see down the track to see if the train might yet be coming but so far there's nothing, and gently but urgently he coaxes the camel to come down and it looks and tramps and then eventually it falters and dropping in a dodder it does. And he turns to show it his ties but the creature just sits there and spits, and the man writhes and tries to explain to it his plight and tries to hearten it to help and in the fullness of his exertion the camel groans and bends and starts with its snout to investigate around him. And it looks and licks and nibbles and sniffs around the man's stomach and then around his neck, and he invites it with nods from his head down to his ankles and arms again to show how he is tied, and the camel ends up nuzzling wetly in his hands and the man aches at the difficulty to communicate and given the proximity of his possible rescue he exasperates.

Then without warning and as if divinely inspired the camel starts gnawing and nibbling on the ties there between the man's wrists and ankles and the track, and it fills its mouth with the plastic and masticates and the man's eyes go wide and he praises God and celebrates the beast and applauds and sings out with hurrahs and hoorays to encourage it on and the camel chows down without rest. And at that juncture the man cranes his head and looks again to see down the track and the moment he does he is dropped to dread and his throat goes dry and his neck turns cold since he sees another blob hovering on the horizon and coming along the track and this time it's there with a deep and terrible rumbling, and then the man feels the ground shake beneath him and the track start to rattle where he is tied and he knows it's the train of his execution come at last to cut him up and he panics and wails and then wills himself back to sense to spur Hosti on.

The camel brings its head up and moans loud and long and then goes back to work munching with streams of slobber and slaver at the man's ankles and arms, and still the train threatens and descends and still the camel chews. And soon the train is not a blob nor hovering but apparent and looming and constant and zooming, and the man sweats and strains and at a sudden moment he feels a change in tensity by his ankles and then with the camel having reached a watershed moment in its chomping he wriggles to help it and the next instant there's a snap and his hands and ankles are away from each other and he can move more loosely or lie back flat, but still he is tied by his feet to the track. And he moves in jerks then to see if he can come free but there's work still to be done so he desperately feeds the camel his wrists and the camel with its fat eyes wild gobbles and dribbles and drools, and it grinds at the cords with its jaw going in circles while the train races forward and rears up to strike and then it is nearly upon them.

And in another instant another cord comes loose and the man then is spare with his hands and he comes round in a crouch and tugs at the remaining tie around his ankles and it stretches and he pulls and yanks at it and jostles and joggles furiously and then he looks up and the train is there large and hard and it sounds out all around with its horn as a portent which fills the camel and man with its blunt and dreadful song, and with that Hosti can take no more and howls and staggers up and skips away to the side and the man tied there cries out and still rushes and then with his final breath and twisting around himself and heaving at the last he comes free and rolls out and not a moment later the train comes through and streaks whizzing between the camel and the man as they scarper in each direction, and they sweat on either side of the train with the camel in stumbles and sways and the man in rolls and then lain flat against the sand, and then the train is past and the man cries in commemoration of his escape and then with trots and jumps from Hosti they're reunited with cheers and nuzzles and tears.

The next moment they're together one on top of the other and galloping east at the peak of their determination to find and get Nadia back, and they go by the way cast by the tracks of the militia's armoured truck which having churned the dirt to be dark as it left has lit a flame

THE MUSLIM COWBOY

by which it might be followed. And they're sweating and their brows are turned down and their pace is urgent and their teeth are showing, and the man's veil from his neck is now made up around his head like a dressing, and there are even some staccato guitars and drums and incantations that come out loud in strums and chants from the dusty black media player docked in the speaker on the back of the saddle rolled and clicked into life by the man to rouse him and his camel as they ride. And going there still reconciled of his two parts and with his Americanness assimilated as part of who he now is, the man thinks with all that and by his old habit of allusion about the Western film *The Searchers*.

And it is an old film by John Ford that stars John Wayne as the war veteran Ethan Edwards who goes with his adoptive nephew Martin Pawley in search of his niece Debbie who is abducted when she is a little girl at the beginning of the film by a tribe of Comanche Indians. He considers that in the film Debbie is missing for years but notes how in the end she is indeed found and saved, and he refers to one scene in particular where the search seems bleak and Ethan tells Marty that if Debbie's still alive then there's a chance that she's safe, and the man takes heart. And then again in his mind's eye he sees Ethan saying how Indians chase a thing until they think they've chased it enough and then they stop, and that it's the same way when they run, as if they don't realise there could be such a thing that could just keep chasing them until they're caught, and then the man is further stirred and he spurs Hosti on to top speed. And so determined there the two of them go, resumed of life and renewed of purpose, and on their way in earnest to a true and suitable ending.

In the fullness of their chase, owing to the weather on the land and the movement of its sand, at some point the man who had been the American and his camel become estranged from the turning trail of impressions left by the armoured truck which steadily disappear beneath them until they're gone, and from then on they keep on its course as well as they can according to the pattern of its path to that part. And at another point thereafter with some time passed since the revitalisation of their mission, and having slept and spent days there in or under the saddle, they grow exhausted of energy and along with that of urgency, and then they're trekking or traipsing and going slower than before though with no less determination.

Soon they come in constancy through the stillness of the desert plain to a proper road of asphalt, and they ride steady to align with it and join it and it bears them still east. On their way along it they see that it meets in the distance with a fuel station beside a small settlement of flat buildings, and since then the sun is high and it is reached about noon they endeavour to stop there and rest. In minutes more they're at the station which is blown out in parts but operative with an attendant and brown from the desert and grey from ash and cratered around, and the attendant says the Muslim greeting and the man who had been the American nods and thinks, and then reconciled in his fullness responds confidently and for the first time in a long time accordingly, that is, with his own Muslim greeting in turn, and then he continues beyond the station to the next building along which is a tea house or rest stop and which stands for the first part of the settlement.

Before the building on the opposite side of the road a woman wrapped in sheets is hanging washing and a young boy beside her is playing with a ball, and as the man goes past them on his camel they barely look up to see. He compares this arrival in his mind to visits he has made previously to other various townships where he has drawn attention or even started fights, and he considers that since he is there now without the apparatus of his Americanness like his hat and jacket, and even having turned off the music on his player for his appearance in silence, he is there only as a man on a camel which isn't in any way extraordinary or odd to the Iraqi eye. He comes to the tea house and brings Hosti prone who though tired moans at not going on, but he settles the animal and then takes his plastic bladders down to refill them and steps the short way to the door.

The tea house is a concrete block with no other structure or stoa, and there are no men sat outside but there are wanted posters on a board the same as at the tea house from before, and they have the same dangerous people on them and the man sees them all and shakes his head and hoists his bladders and walks along. He pushes his way through the door and inside are a few groups of men from different generations scattered around various wooden seats and benches and tables all drinking tea or smoking hookahs. When he enters some look up vaguely and others carry on undisturbed, and the din of chatter there carries on untroubled and is straight, and again the man compares this to the previous times he has entered various tea houses including that last he had been to with Nadia, and this time without hardly any form of acknowledgement he feels a certain sense of liberation and again surmises that it's due to his ordinariness and unadornment.

From the back a standing host with a moustache and a robe of brown and grey comes and says the Muslim greeting and the man who had been the American nods and replies. The host offers tea but the man declines and asks only for water in his bladders and the host bows and assents and leads him to the taps. The other visitors to the house make concessions to move where necessary so the man can take his bladders easily as he and the host go, and when they're at the back and stopped to fill the first bladder the man looks at the host and speaks Arabic to ask him a question, and he says, 'Has any motorcade come through here recently?'

The host looks at him and shrugs and says, 'We see some cars by virtue of having the station for fuel so close,' and the man bows and understands that and looks on, and then looks back at the host and says, 'Any armoured trucks in particular?' And the host says, 'Recently?' And the man says, 'In the last few days,' and the host tilts his head and thinks and taps his moustache and then looks back and says, 'No,' and then, 'Nothing in the last few days,' and the man closes his eyes and curses and then looks up and smiles and says, 'Not to worry.'

The host nods and smiles and then looks out at the room. Soon the first bladder is full, and the host helps to move it and then to bring the second bladder down and they start to fill that too, and while they're waiting the host thinks and

THE MUSLIM COWBOY

then offhandedly speaks, and he says, 'An armoured car like the army would use?' And the man checks his bladder and says, 'Yes,' and the host says, 'Anything like that wouldn't have come this way besides,' and then the host points and says, 'All the army cars take their fuel from the enclosure north of here,' and the man snatches his bladder and then twists to close the tap and his eyes go wide and he looks and says, 'Enclosure?'

The host looks at the man and says, 'The army enclosure, yes,' and the man stands and says, 'What army enclosure?' and, 'Where?' And inspired by the man's urgency the host hurries to speak and says, 'There's an army enclosure north of here where a division lives and trains,' and then, 'You go west down the road and then follow it north,' and the man thinks of the road he and his camel had joined and how they had continued east along it rather than having turned to follow it the other way, and then he is newly with command and charge, and he lifts his bladders and almost spills the first and fullest as he goes, and he thanks the host who says that he is welcome and then stands hurriedly aside.

The man hits a tea drinker on the head with the lighter of his bladders as he goes but even that isn't enough to elicit a response from any of them there who are so heedless of him now that instead of even looking up they just let him leave, and he strafes and tears outside and along to Hosti who shambles and stands once the bladders are fixed to its back and then he jumps and climbs up to its saddle and faces the pair of them west to start at a canter on the way back from where they came. And the man knows that since the Shia militia are in league with the Iraqi Army their best bet at finding the car of their concern should be at the local enclosure so mentioned at the tea house, and like that he and his camel are recalibrated and returned to the road, and like that the two of them proceed.

Having followed the road back they come around the bend of it to go north and soon they come to the turning away from it that leads surely to the army enclosure since there is a sign in blue that admits the path to its location both in Arabic and English and insists that its visitors take a slow and cautious approach as they go. The man who had been the American looks at the sign and ushers Hosti to leave the road there and go a roundabout way through the desert to make an advance entirely of their own so as not to be seen coming, and when the enclosure emerges from over a dune as a big beige block of blast walls the man climbs down from his camel and walks with it to skirt the compound hidden behind the drift, and then they camp out and look around the corner of the bank as far as they can, and from there they are able to spy on it.

Before them is the front of the compound which has smaller blast walls alternating over two lanes before finally a tall red metal gate with a welcome sign above it. Above the gate and the perimeter wall protrude the roofs of all the buildings and rooms of canvas or concrete that are sheltered inside it, along with some tall stone huts that loom as towers to look out over all else. Over and around all those are antennas and stacks of sandbags and then draped netting to cover their various aspects, and in the towers and beneath the welcome sign soldiers of the Iraqi

THE MUSLIM COWBOY

Army are posted in sentry wearing green overalls with short sleeves and claret berets. The man takes note of this all and imagines the number of other soldiers inside all stood or sat about in their berets or otherwise under instruction of exercise or procession or shooting at marks, and he thinks.

Since he is there restrainedly with memories of so many Western films that have cavalry forts in them he lists their names automatically as Worth and Laramie and Bravo and Defiance and Massacre and Petticoat, and then principally he thinks of *Fort Apache* which Nadia had picked out for them to see the night before he had taken her with him after he had first met her in the small town. He thinks of a part in particular where Henry Fonda's character asks Ward Bond's character if he is related to John Agar's character, and they're father and son so Ward Bond's character says that they are, and not by chance but by blood since he's his son, and then the man who had been the American's eyes glaze over and he concludes that if he does feel related to Nadia by now then contrary to that sentiment it is by chance rather than by blood, and then he looks back emphatically at the enclosure and whether sibling or surrogate he is more determined to save her.

He decides to sit and see who might come and go from the gate to discover if the Shia militia from the train might really be using the enclosure as their hideout, and before long there is movement and he engages himself to take heed. It's an arrival from the road and the man looks around the bank as well as he can and then clambers on all fours to the top of his dune to see, and there churning and rumbling on its way to the enclosure is a motorcade of several armoured trucks going along the alternating blast walls like a snake. There's a shout from the berets in sentry and the tall red metal gate screeches and scratches against the dirt to open, and then the man sees inside the enclosure for the first time in earnest and besides the buildings it is mostly stretched wide in a yard, and of course it is crowded with soldiers.

Then the motorcade comes closer and the man sees it completely, and he notes that not only are there men with short sleeved overalls and claret berets like those on sentry at the gate and in the towers of the enclosure, but others in separate trucks at the back with long sleeves and no berets but with black kerchiefs around their necks or pulled over their heads like balaclavas and printed with skulls, and those he knows are Shia militia. And then suddenly at the forefront of one of those trucks as if a tear in the fabric of reality with all his terrible menace is the same captain who took Nadia at the railway, and the smile on his face remains evil and keen and his headband is still silken and dynastic of its green and above it he is still wearing the cowboy hat almost as a souvenir or a medal. And while Nadia is nowhere to be seen the man who had been the American knows that if she still is alive she must be stowed somewhere in the enclosure behind the gate, and then he breathes in summons of strength and hopes that he's not too late.

The trucks go meandering in a line through the gate and the man sees again how differently the soldiers of the militia behave compared to those from the army which is more as a rabble and ruder, and then they're all disappeared inside and the great red gate slams shut with a puff of dust, and once more the enclosure is closed and the soldiers with their berets are stood again in sentry. The man who had been the American reflects and then makes a plan to get in, and nodding to himself soon in sanction of it he comes down beside Hosti and tells the camel to stay there and wait, and then he leaves the dune crawling on his stomach until the berets in sentry are turned away and then he stands and runs stilted and stumbling through the sand to the enclosure's perimeter wall and puts his back to it and breathes.

From there and heading away from the berets at the entrance the man sidesteps around the enclosure to look for another way in but he comes around the whole way without luck, and he looks around the corner and sees the berets at the red gate still sniffing and stepping in the dust and he winces and sighs since through them is the only way in. And he starts on his way back around to double check and to think about what to do next when suddenly there's a bark from a beret in one of the towers and those at the gate jump up and shout back, and the man freezes and throws his hands over his head with the belief he's been seen.

But the shouting continues away from him and it soon becomes clear that he isn't its subject, and curious he creeps back and that's when he notices the cloud. And the berets are all worried and uncertain and shout back and forth to each other between the gate and the tower, and they say puzzled phrases like, 'There's someone coming!' and 'Who is it?' and, 'I can't tell!' And the man still around his corner stands far back enough to look up and see the beret in the tower who is peering through binocular glasses at the horizon where there's the cloud, and those below look up and wait patiently for his verdict but the beret there straining to see for a moment says nothing.

The man below knows the things that clouds like the one before them bring, and he thinks about the things he's seen in his life and how many of them in all of their badness had to do with such clouds making their arrival and imposition on a place or situation, and then his thoughts are interrupted by a call from the beret in the tower who says, 'Are there any motorcades of ours still out?' And the other berets below say, 'No!' And the man in the tower looks still through his glasses and winces to see, and then in the next moment he pulls them down in a panic and looks about with fear in his eyes and says, 'Everyone to their battle stations!' And the berets from below look up and say, 'What?' and, 'Why?' And the one above puts the glasses back to his eyes and strains again to see and then he raises the alarm fully through some system cast behind him and it sounds out loud blaring in a howling clamour around the enclosure, and then he looks down to the berets at the gate and is sympathetic of their position outside and he says, 'It's Sunni militia!'

And the man who had been the American gasps and thinks of the bad men in black overalls who had appeared in the humvee at the small town where he had first met Nadia and then he looks honed at the cloud and shudders, and he defers to the word Nadia had given to those who are about to arrive and speaks it out loud and with dread, and he says, 'Ali Babas!'

The alarm sounds out and there are voices shouting and feet tramping and scrambling in patters all around behind the perimeter wall, and the man who had been the American ventures to run back around to the other side of the enclosure to find Hosti at the dune when he sees in the distance another cloud heading swiftly on its own way to meet them there too, and then he looks out to the side and sees more clouds of motorcades, and he runs around to the other side and sees more there on their way in waves along with the rest and it's clear that the enclosure is to be surrounded in an attack, and the berets in the various towers around the enclosure have seen the other clouds too since then from each of their perches comes commotion and the yard is fallen about in disorder.

The man makes his way back to the entrance where the first cloud is now closer and its source is grown apparent, and he sees that it is a hatchback car coming along the approach's alternating blast walls in kamikaze with a black overalled driver sweating and shouting at the wheel and strapped about his chest with a big rig of bombs. The berets at the gate shout and pray and brace themselves with their rifles held up for impact and send spurts of fire out as they can and the man who had been the American looks with wide eyes and then bleats with fear and runs back around the corner and jumps to cover himself at the last moment before the car arrives and then rifle fire rains down from the towers too but the car finds its mark which is the red metal gate and it rushes over it and explodes with a great flash of light and a bang, and the whole thing is torn apart and the enclosure is rent and in bedlam.

And when he opens his eyes the man who had been the American notices that he has been taken up and thrown by the blast and that there's a great hole where the gate once was. He props himself dizzily on his elbows and rubs his eyes and then looks to the side where there's a rabble of bodies and it's those who were the berets at the gate strewn dashed and derailed from the attack. He looks out into the desert and sees the other distant clouds making their way to hit the enclosure at haste, and then another explosion booms but from the other side of it and there are more shouts and more rattled rounds of rifle fire and then the whole place is under attack.

The man thinks of Nadia hidden somewhere inside and decides to take advantage of the event, and wincing he clambers crouched to his feet so he can see beyond the mangled gate and into the yard. Through the cloud of dust he sees the towers and buildings and rooms and then an open barracks and canvas mess with beds and desks to boot, and he shakes his head to sense and stumbles through and then he is swiftly within. There's another smoking hole in the perimeter wall at the far end of the enclosure to which many soldiers with their green overalls and claret berets are running mixed with militia in panic and shouting with their rifles in the air, and then there's another boom to the side and another hole appears from another car having come accursedly against it in kamikaze, and the soldiers run through more dust to meet that too. The man looks on as two black humvees rush through the new hole in billows bringing with them hails of flak and fire spewed from mounted guns that meet soldiers of all stripes who are taken down in turn, and the man jumps behind a pile of sandbags close to the canvas mess as shots come over his head. He sits there and thinks again of Nadia and cries with the desire to reach her, and with the circumstance of the attack now he feels entirely helpless.

In the yard men in black overalls scramble down from the humvees and scatter and take hidden positions against the berets and militia who find themselves staked in their own turn and then they all on either side rattle rifle fire over each other as they can. The man who had been the American cowers behind his sandbags until there's yet another boom which sends another cloud of dust into the air and makes another hole in the perimeter wall somewhere so near that it exposes his hiding place, and then there's another boom further down and on the opposite side. And with so many holes now in the wall another wave arrives of more black humvees which pull dust and ride firing into the yard, and more men in black overalls come down and run and shoot and some of them are belted and stuffed like the one in the hatchback car with explosives and those run and scream and burst purposely on buildings, and the attack comes from all sides and is violent and relentless.

And the man looks about covered in dust and winces and crouches with ringing in his ears and then stumbles along as he can to the mess which is now torn with its canvas all flapping around and he tries to find refuge within, and he goes ducked and hopping over trodden berets and battered bodies and staggers with wide eyes past skirmishes wrestled by hand between green and black overalled men until he comes to the end of the mess and looks out to the next building which he sees then is a hangar. And it's unlike the other rooms of the enclosure in that it's made not from concrete but of steel and it's open and intact still, and that rather than an arena for the fray it's instead become one for escape since inside are various militia men who have given up on the scope to fight back and are competing to seize the armoured trucks that are parked there so they can retreat and leave at short haste.

The man stops and looks urgently into the hangar through its opening as some militia men approach one of the closer trucks and watches as a brave beret soldier alone accosts them and dictates that they should stay and strike back. The militia men laugh in turn but sweating then too from their panic push past the beret and throw him to the floor and climb into the truck, and one of them at the front turns the key in its console to enkindle its engine and it rasps and then he rolls the stick for its gears and it purrs and then roars but in the next instant the beret is back up and there again shouting, and he curses and says strong words like, 'Traitors!' and, 'Snakes!'

And still shouting the beret comes through the door to pull the closest man back out from the van but then without warning there's a loud crack and a shot that comes to the top of his head which pops and comes open with bits of skull and his blood, and his beret falls with a hole in it to the side and his body falls limp and is pushed out and away. And the man who had been the American looks on from the flapping mess as then from behind the side of the opening comes a militia man in particular walking with two others and a hand outstretched with a smoking gun which is the colt revolver, and his headband is silken and green beneath the cowboy hat on his head, and there's a girl in an oversized denim jacket struggling and screaming with his hand around her wrist. And there at last and the same as she ever was only now covered in dust and so close to her deliverance is Nadia, and the man who had been the American cries out wholeheartedly and burns, and arrived then at the opportunity of her rescue his stomach turns. And having been brought to his charge he knows that if he's ever to save her then this would be his chance, and he looks at the yard from the mess for the risk and then there's a boom and a cloud, and with the dust there to cover him and without thinking anything further he shouts to be bold and then he runs out.

The militia captain with the green headband has Nadia lifted by the wrist to haul her up to his comrades in the truck when the man who had been the American emerges suddenly at the hangar through the dusted mist and casts a closed fist at his smiling face to bop it, and the headband man is caught unawares and struck on his cheek and then dealt with a second punch that comes thrown up from under his chin with a bang, and he flies back from the blows and lands on the floor and the cowboy hat falls away from his head and Nadia in her smallness is tossed to one side.

And Nadia looks up sore from the floor and for the first time since the railway she sees her friend and screams with glee and she says, 'You came!' And the man who had been the American growls with his hands still up showing his knuckles to spar on and says, 'Of course I did,' and he looks at the headband man out cold and collapsed on the floor and then at the truck with its skull faced militia men left there bewildered and looking on, and then he reaches out to Nadia and says, 'We have to leave,' and she brings herself around and says, 'Are we going to Jordan?' And he says, 'I don't know,' and he looks and says, 'But wherever it is, we'll go there together,' and Nadia beams bright and her eyes go wide and she says, 'Together as friends?' And the man looks at her then and is sure and nods and he says, 'Together as friends,' and the two of them reconciled both sob from their happiness.

And Nadia gets up and runs to go with him but suddenly she chokes and stops and is clasped around the neck and then clutched by her scruff, and it's the headband man who has come around and stood back up. And there's a boom from beyond the hangar and the flash from it clarifies the silken stripe around his head which has slipped to sit at an angle but which from the light seems now to shine out greener than ever, and he holds Nadia tight with his arm around her neck and her chin at his elbow and blood runs red from his nose and he licks it, and then he looks at the man who had been the American and he spits and says, 'You,' and then, 'The Hater man here to find his Hater girl.' And he tightens his hold around Nadia's neck and she gasps, and then he gestures rudely and through his nose to the black overall men outside and he sneers and looks at the man who had been the American and says, 'No doubt you arrived here with your Hater friends who must have found you at the railway,' and he smiles and is sick and his teeth are red from his blood.

And then a rattle of rifle fire comes in patters with great clangs against the side of the hangar and everyone looks up, and the skulled troop in the truck who are the headband man's comrades and who have been waiting for him grow skittish and their driver is anxious and impatient and without further ado rips at the engine in rolls and brings the truck around the headband man and Nadia in jerks and then bolts past the man who had been the American and races out from the hangar through its opening and out from the enclosure through a bombed hole and away into the desert east to where the other militia men all seem to be fleeing, and the headband man stands there deserted and says, 'Cowards!' And then he looks around with a grimace at the few trucks still left and being filled and he says, 'Never mind,' and, 'I'll take another truck!' And then he snatches at Nadia to reset his hold on her.

And with time running out the man who had been the American steps forward and sweats and says, 'Let her go,' and, 'Let us be,' but even at the suggestion of his assertion the headband man brings up and holds the colt on him and is cruel and sick again with his smile, and Nadia twists and turns in a panic and the headband man tugs at her to be still and then he spits again and says, 'I should leave you both here,' and, 'You've been too much trouble already,' and two more trucks then roar and leave past him, and the headband man says, 'But why deign to leave you and retreat when I can shoot you?' And the man who had been the American winces but is determined and steps forward again and then the headband man says, 'Perhaps it's a more fitting end even than the railway for you to have been shot with a revolver, cowboy.'

And with an eye closed then he takes aim and Nadia is distraught and cries out and says, 'No!' And the headband man is ruthless and shoots, and there's a crack and a clang and the man who had been the American flies back and falls and in the next instant is laid down on the dust at the mouth of the hangar prostrate and passed entirely from his personality and from presence, and all around trucks are roaring and rifles are firing and the rage and the fury of everything rings on.

Nadia stands apprehended with the green headband man's arm still stiff around her neck and looks at the body of her friend listless and limp with its eyes shut, and her eyes in turn are wide and her mouth is dropped open and then a sob comes unwanted from her throat and tears run down her cheeks and all told she is speechless and in shock. And she is tugged around by the headband man and goes dragged with him in a circle quiet and numb like a block as he looks for a truck until in an instant and with a jump she is brought back by a boom which reinserts with its advent everything else of the upheaval outside the hangar and in the yard and then she finds fully her despair at what she has lost and is dazed and disturbed and distraught.

And she looks craning as she can up to see her abductor and he is there wheezing and bleeding all of bitterness and bile with his headband now tilted, and he looks this way and that in flits to find some car he can confiscate but so many of them now have been claimed. And looking up at him she thinks how he has murdered her friend and how it was for what she previously had been told about as a schism in their country which is the separation of Haters and Rejectors and she thinks of where she had first heard about that which had been at Ali's and then she thinks of another thing she had learnt there which with urgency she applies to her situation now, and it was a thing that Ali himself had made known and it was that if God ever gives you a test then you have two choices which are either to fight or to flee, and that of those two you must pick one because either to fight or to flee is better than to freeze.

And with that and the fate of her friend in her mind and even in her loneliness now she endeavours to go on, and then it's after the example of one of her friend's old Western films that she finds the formula for it and the film is *True Grit* which she had seen at Ali's and the scene is that in which the girl Mattie Ross gets away from the gatekeeper who is guarding her to gallop downstream and ford the river on the back of her submerged horse so she can join Rooster Cogburn and the ranger LaBoeuf on the other side, and Nadia remembers that Mattie had done that by catching the gatekeeper off guard and then swiping him across the face with her hat, and she looks around and sees the cowboy hat of her friend down in the dust where it had fallen once the headband man had been forced before to the floor, but stuck under the headband man's arm she is unable to reach it and she struggles against him but is left wanting and then winces, and then she thinks more.

And she looks at her own situation and determines to apply the same technique in her own way, and she thinks about how Mattie speaks to the gatekeeper to distract him before she hits him by saying that she ought to fix her hat, and then Nadia stops struggling and speaks to the headband man in her own turn, and she says, 'You ought to fix your headband.'

And the headband man hears her and at so pointed a message stops in surprise and says, 'What?' And she repeats herself and then he reaches up to his headband and notices that it's become sloped, and he ventures to straighten it and as he does Nadia is relinquished in part from his grip and in that moment she twists her head and chomps on his arm with her teeth and then stomps on his feet with her heels as hard as she can and he cries out in some pain but mostly in surprise and he unhands the colt and his headband falls over his eyes.

And then Nadia is let go and she gets away altogether, and she darts down to the ground to find the colt and then has it in her hands and she lifts it with a wince and then turns it on the headband man, and he pulls his headband up from his eyes and sees her there in her oversized jacket and red with anger and alarm, and he looks and laughs and then speaks with a sneer and says, 'Hater girl you don't know how to use that,' and Nadia stood there thinks again of *True Grit* and the part when Mattie has found Tom Chaney at last and threatens him with her own gun and Chaney is haughty and tells her that she'd better cock the hammer all the way back until it locks, and then she moves and is quick, and she brings the gun to her chest and strains to bring its hammer back with all her fingers and in an instant it clicks and then the headband man cries out and has rushed her and is there with his eyes wide open and grabbing in panic and she screams and then fires and she flies back in one way and he flies in the other and then he falls and she looks and he is laid out in darkness with a hole between his eyes which are blank and unblinking and rolled partly in dust, and it's clear that he is dead and Nadia sits there and is numb.

And she looks at the gun still heavy in her hand and then drops it and whimpers and then she breathes fast from the stress of what she's done and the headband man's face pools with blood and she sees it and sits there and shakes and she cries. And the remaining trucks go past all around her and leave the hangar and then outside there's a final explosion and Nadia looks up and around and then she stumbles and stands with a sob. She looks out into the yard and sees a man in green overalls crawl bleeding along the floor and then she sees one in black overalls walk up and execute the green one with a shot in the back and she gasps and pushes herself in hiding against the hangar wall. She looks down at the body of the headband man and then she sees that of her friend, and he's there with his jeans and his boots and his cowboy hat trodden flat on the side and then her knees go weak and she staggers to see him but the moment she comes away from the wall a large figure steps into her path.

She looks up and stood there is the strong man who she and the man who had been the American had seen in the humvee in her small town with his light skin and black robe and short hair and rimless glasses and black boots and glock handgun and bullet-proof vest hung on his shoulders and open for his chest, and Nadia remembers him and winces, and he looks down at her through his glasses with his eyes vacant and glazed and then speaks calmly, and he says, 'Who are you?' And he looks past her at the colt on the floor and then at headband man's body and then at that of the man who had been the American, and then he looks back at Nadia and he says, 'Little girl,' and, 'What are you doing here?'

Nadia whimpers but finds it hard to answer and the strong man walks around her and she turns with him. He approaches the dead headband man and looks down at his body and then looks back at Nadia scared as she is and then back to the body, and he says, 'You shot him,' and then, 'Tell me your name.' And Nadia looks at the strong man and whimpers and blinks, and finally she says, 'Nadia,' and the strong man looks at her and says, 'You are Sunni?' And she nods and says, 'Yes.' And the strong man looks at the body of the headband man and says, 'God is good,' and then he spits on the body and says, 'He was a Rejector,' and then he looks at Nadia and smiles and says, 'He was not like you and me.'

Nadia's eyes widen then and her eyebrows raise and she says, 'I'm not like you,' and, 'You're Ali Babas,' and the strong man looks at her and laughs and says, 'We're not Ali Babas,' and Nadia says, 'You fight people and kill them!' And the strong man laughs again and then raises his eyebrows, and he gestures to the dead body of the headband man and says, 'If you define it like that then we're both Ali Babas,' and Nadia winces and shakes her head and lowers her eyes, and then with gravity the strong man says, 'No,' and then, 'We are the soldiers of the Prophet, and God willing we are coming.'

Then the strong man approaches the colt on the floor and looks at it and then he looks away and speaks again, and he says, 'You can come with us Nadia,' and Nadia looks at the strong man with her eyebrows upturned and worry on her face, then she looks at the body of the headband man and then she turns and looks the body of the man who had been the American who had been her friend, and she thinks of him and is sad to her stomach at their severance and she sobs.

And she wants to go and see him and be with him and help to bury him like he helped to bury her mother, but the strong man is there then with his hand out to her and unrelenting. And she looks at the strong man and then at the trodden cowboy hat of her friend on the floor and she thinks about the film *Shane* and remembers watching it for the first time and wearing that hat and she remembers Shane and his speech to little Joe Starrett before he leaves when he says that there's no going back from a killing and that it's a brand and moreover a brand that sticks, and then she looks at the dead body of the headband man again and covers her face with her hands and she thinks that now she might never be able to grow up to be straight like Shane says.

And then she looks again at the strong man, and she thinks that if she is taken to go with the Ali Babas she might at least grow up to be strong which is the other of Shane's recommendations for Joe, and she looks again at the body of her friend and thinks that if nothing else if she goes with the Ali Babas she might survive, and she remembers that to survive alone or in company for her friend had been the point of everything anyway.

And gradually there and sick of heart Nadia reconciles herself with what she feels she must based on what she thinks she knows, and eventually she turns to the strong man and says, 'Where are you going?' And he looks at her, and then she says, 'Are you going west to Jordan?' And the strong man studies her and then says, 'No,' and then he says, 'We're going north to Syria,' and Nadia looks at the floor. And she plays with the cuffs on her oversized denim jacket and then looks at the body of her friend, and then with a thought she says, 'Are there Americans in Syria?' And the strong man looks at her and raises his eyebrows, and then a smile comes over his face and he says, 'Yes,' and then as if under a shadow he says, 'There are many Americans in Syria.' And Nadia looks again at the body of her friend and then again at the strong man, and the strong man looks deeply at her and again he holds out his hand and is quiet and patient, and this time she looks at it and relents, and she takes it, and they go.

When the man wakes up everything is quiet and dark, and he lies there and his head is pounding and he's barely able to breathe and then he remembers the enclosure and he remembers Nadia and in Arabic he says, 'Oh man...' And he wrestles to become untangled from whatever it is under which he's been covered and it gesticulates in lumps and swells in the dust until he emerges from it and breathes gasping at the silent air there in the open hangar.

He thinks back and remembers having been fired at by the green headband man and then looks about his body for where the shot may have hurt him. He touches his head and arms in a panic but everywhere he goes to feels well, then he pats down his front and in the centre of his chest comes with his hands over the golden star badge from the limited package of his colt that he had stuck to his T-shirt at the edge of the desert after he and Nadia had been through the abandoned old city. Sure enough it has the providential shot from the colt lodged between the letters of the word

THE MUSLIM COWBOY

'Sheriff', and the man looks forward blankly and then looks to the ceiling and gives thanks to God and he breathes.

Then he lifts up what had been covering his face and sees that it's his old denim jacket, and he looks at it and thinks and then with wide eyes he says, 'Nadia,' and he stands and staggers and looks around for her in the hangar which is half blown out and burnt. He sees only three things there which are the tossed colt and the cowboy hat and then the dead body of the headband man on the floor, and he looks closer and sees the body then with its hole in the head and blood all around, and then he looks at the tossed colt and the hat, and then he looks between all three and stands there and thinks and he stares and he blinks.

And then there are bangs and rumbles and roars from somewhere beyond the hangar and the man looks up and all around and again he says, 'Nadia,' and he stumbles out from the hangar to the yard and looks around and sees it strewn as it is with bodies and berets along with so many dark craters in the floor and holes around the perimeter wall, and most of the buildings there are collapsed including the torn mess and the towers, and plastics and rubble are peppered all over and patches of soot and strips of fire are still burning or in embers and dust is hanging in the air and smoke is rising to the sky, and then there are more rumbles and roars and through one of the holes to the desert comes a motorcade of black humvees from the side and it churns and thunders and then swings around and sends dust into the air and begins to ride frenzied in a hum away from the enclosure and north into the desert, and the man runs out through the hole in the perimeter wall after it.

The motorcade makes its way in a clamour and kicks behind it a great big dust cloud and when the man is outside he stops and waves the dust from the air with his arms and then looks. And moment to moment there are windows in the cloud and through each of them he sees in flashes the blackness of its riders' overalls stood as they are in the beds of its trucks, and then with wide eyes he sees among them the strong man from the humvee in the small town where he met Nadia and from the laminated posters at the tea houses in the hamlet and the fuel station, and he is there with his black robe and vest and his glock at the forefront of the riders and they're all with their backs to the man at the enclosure who looks anxiously between them in darts.

And then in a flash he sees along with them a small face behind the cloud, and it's Nadia, and he thinks for an instant that she sees him back but he is too shocked even to shout out and then the dust billows up and the window is closed and they are split, and when another flash comes he sees her turned like the rest in the trucks and there's only the back of her head through the cloud and then the dust comes up and this time hangs large churned now as it is from the ground with the gathered speed from the wheels of the trucks, and then they're out of clear range and there's only the big cloud and below it vaguely the blackness of what has made it, and then it is like all the other clouds from before, that is, undefined and of a motorcade and moving quickly but this time in flight unlike and opposite to those others that had seemed always to be in an endless state of approach.

And when the motorcade is barely manifest and the cloud is moved away from the enclosure the man looks at the oversized denim jacket that Nadia had been wearing for the most recent half of their journey and which she must have left over his face in ceremony or as if in display, and then he looks at the cloud again and he frowns. And a wind blows, and the man looks to the east and there is the cloud of another motorcade though smaller than the other and he can see distantly that the riders' overalls of that one are green and then he looks at the denim jacket again and then north once more at the black cloud, and then he turns back to the enclosure and looks at that.

And then alone there he lifts the denim jacket again and looks at it with mournful wretched eyes. And then he looks at it with blank eyes. And then without thinking he beats it for dust and brings his arms through the sleeves, and if he had been renewed before on the railway he begins now the process of being folded over and pressed from himself for a second time and this time maybe even more so than the first. And then absently he pulls his veil down from his head where it had been as a dressing and ties it around his neck and he brings his vape pen up from his pocket and fills it anew with a vial left over from his jacket and he activates it and draws heavily from it the flavour of apple and drinks it down and holds it in and his head then is filled and made fuzzy again.

And enveloped there and then he thinks again about the Western film *The Searchers* and a part in particular when the mother of Marty's love interest Laurie talks about being what she calls a Texican living where she does, and he hears her speak in her old voice about how a Texican is a human who exists out on a limb from one year to the next and who could exist maybe for a hundred years, and then he hears her say how she doesn't think Texicans will exist forever since someday where they live will be a fine and good place to be and how maybe it just needs their bones in the ground before that time can come. And then the man leans with his back against the perimeter wall and he looks out from there into the desert.

And in the fullness of time he is joined by Hosti who arrives nodding and who is constant and unremitting and moaning, and the man greets the beast and snores from his pen a honeyed mist and it floats up in trickles from his nostrils and over his eyes, and the motorcade recedes with its cloud in the north and the sun makes its descent to the horizon in the west and casts long shadows across the plain as the air turns cold. And the motorcade is gone but its cloud is still there small in the distance when the man finally turns away and walks in dead parade with his camel back into the open enclosure which by now is a square of long clotted shadows.

And they go from there into the hangar and the man looks for his hat and finds it where it had been left, and he lifts it and punches it out from flatness and places it on his head and then with his forefinger propelled from behind his thumb he flicks the front of its brim and it lands halfway up his forehead. Then he turns and goes some steps and bends and takes up the colt, and he clicks at his camel and it is dutiful and promptly goes prone, and then the man is stretched of that same old yawn from those other times before that comes up from the bottom of his stomach, and he tilts his head down and looks at the floor and winces and closes his eyes and breathes in with a draw. And then all at once he vaults the camel and lands deep in its saddle and brings it up, and it comes with a great heave forward and back and then totters until it stands heavy and level and it moans, and the man there atop it in his own turn is focused and honed.

And with his head bowed the man jams the colt snout down in the back of his jeans with its black handle in a hook over his waistband and then helps the camel along with his heels, and breathing slowly and softly he brings them both out from under the hangar into the desert. And one last time he looks out north at the diminishing cloud there on the horizon, and he glances too at the smaller one east, and then he takes the camel and he faces it west. And he narrows his eyes and takes a final deep breath and then he grips the strings of the camel's reins and squeezes its saddle well with his thighs, and then without warning he hits its hump with his free hand in a slap and it stands, and suspended there on its back legs it moans and the man roars. And then he shouts loud a last charge and the camel is fired and runs, and the man rides out flown from there as the American into the immortal setting sun.

ACKNOWLEDGEMENTS

Thank you especially to Charles Saatchi, Caroline Michel, and Tim Binding. Thank you also to Kieron Fairweather, Francesca Morgan, Laurie Robertson, and everyone else at Peters Fraser and Dunlop; Harriet Hirshman, Nathan Connolly, Gary Budden, Nathaniel Ashley, Emma Ewbank, and the team at Dead Ink; and Fiona McMorrough, Emma Mitchell, Kealey Rigden, Ned Green, and everyone else at FMcM. Thank you also to Sammy Sultan, Ian Endfield, Luca Galbiati, Jack Edwards, Rory DCS, and Raf Seneviratne. Not least of all, thank you to my mother and the rest of my family, especially Hatty, Arthur, Phoebe, Danny, and little Daphne.

ABOUT THE AUTHOR

Bruce Omar Yates was born in London to an Indian mother and an English father. He grew up in the south of France before returning to London to study Literature and Film at King's College London. He was principal songwriter in the rock groups Famy, who released their album *We Fam Econo* in 2014, and Los Porcos, who released their album *Porco Mio* in 2016. *The Muslim Cowboy* is his first novel.

About Dead Ink

Dead Ink is a publisher of bold new fiction based in Liverpool. We're an Arts Council England National Portfolio Organisation.

If you would like to keep up to date with what we're up to, check out our website and join our mailing list.

www.deadinkbooks.com | @deadinkbooks